...anted

...m at

...se in

..., and

...t.

Also in the Contents series

Also by Keith Gray

Creepers
Hunting the Cat (from May 1997)

Contents

KEITH GRAY

FROM BLOOD
TWO BROTHERS

mammoth

First published in Great Britain 1997
by Mammoth an imprint of Reed International Books Ltd
Michelin House, 81 Fulham Road, London SW3 6RB
and Auckland, Melbourne, Singapore and Toronto

ISBN 0 7497 2768 3

A CIP catalogue record for this title is available
from the British Library

Printed and bound in Great Britain
by Cox & Wyman Ltd, Reading, Berkshire

this one's for steve
my friend, and my accomplice, throughout the years
(and while we're chasing summer, we'll forever be here
inside spring)

PART ONE

Chapter One

It's weird how basically it all began with thoughts of blood.

I was sitting there thinking that maybe, just maybe, I had actually managed to find a way to crawl inside one of my own veins. After all, everything was the right colour: red. Everything in the room was tinted red. The usually pallid light bulb had been replaced by a scarlet coloured one and the room was bathed in gore from skirting board to ceiling. The cigarette smoke eddied almost imperceptibly, it seemed somehow fluid, suffused a deep crimson. And there was even a definite pulse. 120 bpm. The repetitive rhythmn of a dance record pumping its bass that little bit quicker than my real heart.

I pushed my glasses up my nose and squinted down at the empty bottle of Thunderbird lying at my feet. Cheap. Potent. It complemented the atmosphere perfectly.

I was slumped in a hugely cushioned settee waiting for Paul to return from the toilet. A few people swam past me through the fog of the living room, heading for the kitchen. I hid the bottle of Southern Comfort I'd found in the washing machine behind my back, feeling

1

guilty. They all returned with cans and bottles of beer and I consoled myself that it probably wasn't their own either. They headed back into the hallway and the dining room beyond. That was where the main party seemed to be happening, but at the moment I was quite content with letting the over-soft settee suck at me.

I glanced quickly across at the opposite wall. I grinned. She was still there, sitting cross-legged leaning back against the wall, concentrating hard on the Gameboy in her hands.

We weren't the only ones in the living room however. There was a lower-sixth kid, fag always on the go, who seemed to have taken control of the stereo. I wasn't over keen on the music, I'd never been much of a dance fan really (Paul and I had already ferreted through the CDs in search of something decent but had come up blank). And then the kid insisted on making it worse by changing the records before they were properly finished. One wouldn't even be halfway through before he'd swap it for another. The songs changed but the beat remained the same, and I suppose that was all that mattered really.

Andy Briggs was also here. Rachael Mumby too. They were squashed tightly into the far corner of the room underneath the bay window. The curtains were drawn and it was hard to see them through the smoke. I would have opened the window to get rid of the stuff if it hadn't been for them. He had a hand, she had a breast. I didn't want to have to climb over them.

And sitting opposite, snoring in an armchair, a snailish trail of dribble down one side of his chin, was the party's host, Mathew Harker. He'd been out of it since about nine, even though he'd spilt most of what he'd been drinking. He was eighteen today, and a very happy birthday to him too. His parents had gone out for the evening and they'd said he could have a few friends round if he wanted. But Matty Harker, being Matty Harker, had invited practically the whole of the sixth form. And then those not invited had turned up anyway. Not that Matty cared, he was good like that. You could always rely on him for a laugh. Paul and I had already filled his open mouth with cat hair and fluff from underneath the settee, but had tired of the game after he'd swallowed his second gobful and our Thunderbird had dried up.

This was quite possibly the last party of the year, definitely the last party of the sixth form. Today had also been the last day of the exams (Sociology and English – I think I rushed my English paper, but who cared? now I was FREE!), and from now on we'd be going to parties as university students. Or at least that was the plan. We'd just have to wait and see what the results had to say about that one, but most of us were confident. Most of us. Even Paul.

He wandered back into the living room, screwing his eyes up against the smoke, still fiddling with the fly button on his Magical Pulling Pants. They were his favourite pair; pinstriped.

'Have you seen the state of the bathroom?' he asked, plopping himself down next to me on the settee. 'Man, it's really gross.' He shook his head. 'No, no, it's worse than gross. It's . . .' and he made a repulsive, deep-throated, retching noise.

I nodded. It was. I brandished the stolen bottle of Southern Comfort. 'Look what I found in the washing machine,' I grinned.

Paul took it off me. 'Smart,' he said, and promptly broke the seal.

As he took the first mouthful I glanced again at the girl with the Gameboy. And it was okay, she was still there. I watched her for a little while, safe in the knowledge that she was concentrating too hard on her game to notice me staring at her. I saw her swear under her breath. I guessed she'd died then. She had fair hair that fell to just below her chin, parted down the middle, kind of bobbed, and she tucked it behind her ears as she shifted her position, pulling her knees up in front of her so she could rest the little console against her thighs. She took a quick swig from a bottle of Bud by her side. She was wearing cherry-red DM shoes. She had a hole in the knee of her jeans where I could just glimpse some pale skin. She shuffled on her backside, making herself comfy, then settled down to concentrate on her game again.

Paul nudged me and I realised he was talking to me.

'Eh? What?'

'You're not listening are you?'

I was offended. 'Yeah, I am.' I took the Southern Comfort from him and had myself a good swig. It was sickly sweet, like week-old jelly babies left out on your bedroom windowsill.

'So, what d'you reckon then?' Paul asked.

'About what?'

'I thought you said you were listening.'

'I am.'

'You weren't though.'

'But I am *now*.' I offered him the bottle and a smile.

He tutted. 'You really wind me up sometimes, you know,' he told me.

I grinned, and pushed my glasses up my nose, catching another glimpse of the girl with the Gameboy.

We were old friends, Paul and I, we'd been through most of school together. We'd met when I first moved to Cleeston Comprehensive and had been pretty much inseparable ever since. Paul had had really bright blond hair back then, Milky Bar Kid stuff, but over his teenage years it had darkened to become what you could only just call fair. He still doted on it though; the only thing to be seen with him more often than me was his hairbrush. He was trying to grow it long at the moment, trying to get it into a ponytail. And it would go. Just. If forced. He was a tall kid, trim, not skinny like me, and not bad looking in a boyish kind of way, I suppose. I guess it was his eyes; too bright to hold many worries, always a mischievous gleam. And he still didn't need to shave, or at least not beyond his top lip anyway, which I guess also helped to keep the girls calling him 'cute'.

'I was talking about Jane Lois-Lane,' he told me. 'She's here, and she's looking *gorgeous*.'

'But nothing like Lois Lane,' I said.

'Yeah she does, can't you tell?'

'She's got the same hairstyle, and that's it.'

'And her eyes, don't forget her eyes. You can tell if you look her in the eyes.' Paul took another mouthful of somebody else's Southern Comfort. 'It's definitely in her eyes.'

I let the matter drop; it was an old argument. But trust me, she looked no more like Lois Lane than my mum did. Less even.

'You do realise she goes out with Bob Moody, don't you?'

He dismissed the fact with a shrug.

'Well, it's your lookout.'

'Yeah, I know. But she's so nice. And I don't know about you,' he winked at me, 'but personally I fancy moseying on through for a bit of Steady Progress in the dining room.'

I shrugged. 'In a minute,' I said. I turned my gaze to the girl with the Gameboy. 'Do you know who she is?'

Paul shook his head. 'No idea, who is she?'

'Dunno. That's why I asked you.'

'Never seen her before.' He paused for a swig. 'She's nice though.'

I nodded. 'Very.'

We sat in silence watching her, swapping the bottle back and forth. She died and started swearing again. She couldn't have been any good at computer games.

I've always found an attractive woman to be kind of a social thing. You can see it in the street; the turn of men's heads as a pretty girl passes by. And it happened here, too. Joe and Mike Dunnery waded into the smoky living room coming from the kitchen, carrying a six-pack each, chatting. They both noticed the girl with the Gameboy, and both cast admiring glances in her direction. Then noticed us noticing them, and her; smiles and raised eyebrows were passed between us. We didn't usually get on with the Dunnery brothers, but in that brief moment the girl with the Gameboy brought the four of us together, in mutual admiration of her good looks.

'Somebody must know who she is,' I said.

Paul shrugged. 'I dunno. I mean, she's not with anybody is she? It doesn't look as if she's got any mates here.'

'Maybe I should go over and talk to her,' I said. 'Introduce myself. Give her some company. She might be lonely.'

Paul nodded. 'Go on then.'

I took a hefty mouthful of Southern Comfort. And I almost stood up. Honest.

'Nar,' I said. 'She's probably waiting for someone.'

'I'll talk to her for you,' Paul offered.

I grabbed his shirt sleeve. 'No! Don't! It doesn't matter.'

He grinned hugely at me. 'I don't mind,' he said. 'Trust me. I'll say nice things about you.' But he had that certain twinkle in his eye and I remembered how he'd humiliated me all those years ago with Lisa Horner from my maths group. I shook my head, holding his shirt sleeve tight. And he laughed at me. 'Chicken.'

I had yet another swig from the pilfered bottle. 'She's out of my league anyway. She wouldn't be interested in me,' I said, hoping Paul would argue.

But instead he nodded. 'Yeah, probably wouldn't want some speccy git like you disturbing her game.'

I laughed. 'So you reckon she probably prefers the ones with pretend long hair, do you?'

'Probably.'

'Yeah.'

I gave her one last glance. But it grew into a stare. One day, I told myself, one day. Maybe. If I was lucky. If I could somehow catch her off guard, surprise her, sneak up on her when she wasn't looking, when she was least expecting it.

I've always maintained that you've got to be strategic, you've got to use tactics. But it's more like a war than a game of football. You've got to be able to plan your manoeuvres with military precision. You've got to know where and how to break through their lines of defence. Not that I myself have ever had much success admittedly . . . Perhaps I needed a bigger tank.

Paul nudged me. 'Come on,' he said. 'Let's go through and talk to Jane.' And so we did. Taking somebody else's bottle of Southern Comfort with us, half-empty now.

The dining room was chocker, bodies everywhere, and the smoke was much thicker than in the living room. But at least everything was the right colour. Someone had pushed the table back against the far wall and perched its six chairs rather precariously on top. Jane Lois-Lane had neatly ensconced herself beneath the table; Paul spotted her, and we made our way over. I stood on at least three hands, kicked a couple of feet, but luckily managed not to spill anybody's beer. I could feel my own alcohol thick in my head. I knew that when you swallowed it was supposed to drain down into your stomach, whereas for me it definitely felt as if it had somehow swirled its way upwards to fill my head, making it way too heavy on top of my feeble neck. I apologised profusely as I stumbled my way across the room and let out a little sigh of relief as I crawled beneath the massive table to join Paul, Jane Lois-Lane and her mate, Laura.

Paul and Jane Lois-Lane (who still looked nothing like Superman's top tottie to me, even after all that I'd been drinking) immediately leapt into conversation. Laura lit up a fag and ignored me, which was fine because I'd never liked her either. She was wearing a white, cropped T-shirt with the word BABE emblazoned across the chest. It was a lie. She reckoned she was hard because she had an older boyfriend in the RAF called Doug. So I leaned back against the wall, my head ducked so it didn't hit against the underside of the table, and nursed the Southern Comfort (which Paul seemed to have forgotten about, now that Jane Lois-Lane was sharing her cider with him).

I watched the others in the room, my friends from school, as they shared jokes and cigarettes, playing drinking games, chatting. It struck me that these were the same people who had been so tense and hassled and worried for the last few months, stressed out over their exams. I took a swig from my bottle and silently wished them all the best of luck. I reckoned that if their papers had been anything like mine then they certainly needed it. And I smiled, my chin resting on my chest, feeling rather charitable, benevolent even. So I didn't feel in the least bit bad as I wigged in on Paul and Jane's conversation.

'No, honestly, I really like it. It looks good on you.'

'It's not too short?'

'As if. You've got great legs. Best to show them off.'

A giggle. 'My dad says it's too short.'

A shrug. 'What do dads know? Mine reckons my hair's too long.'

'I like lads with long hair. Are you growing yours much longer?'

'As long as I can.' There was a brief pause, then he said: 'Do you know who you remind me of . . .?'

I switched off at that point. It looked like Paul was in there anyway, making plenty of Steady Progress. And I reckoned that was exactly what I should have been doing. I should have been out and about, mingling with the women. I should have been back in the living room talking to the girl with the Gameboy . . .

And once again I *almost* stood up. But I guess basically, when it came down to it, I simply didn't have the guts. I wasn't able to walk up to girls and immediately start talking to them. Unlike Paul. Paul could hold a conversation with just about anybody saying just about anything. ('I reckon my hair might get tangled in my cape though. You know, if I was Superman.') And I wasn't like that.

I cuddled up to the bottle, feeling completely sorry for myself. I felt like I was sitting in my own personal exclusion zone: no chat or laughter here! I took a mouthful of Southern Comfort. Maybe I'd be able to talk to her in a couple of minutes.

But the minutes dragged, my head got heavier and heavier, and the bottle became lighter. Paul's sweet-talk, the music seeping through from the living room and Jane Lois-Lane's giggles all merged together to form some kind of bizarre but soothing lullaby. I closed my eyes and fell asleep sitting upright underneath the dining room table.

Big mistake.

I woke with a start, cracking my head on the underside of the table, and immediately knew I was going to puke.

Everybody in the room was looking at me; they'd all crowded around the table. They were all laughing. I tried to scramble out from where I was trapped, pushing and shoving at the people clogging up my escape route. Didn't they realise what I was about to do? Did they want it down their new shirts? I was holding my breath, trying to keep it in. Jets of saliva sprayed the inside of my mouth. Any second now, any second . . .

I made it to the door, and burst through into the hallway. There was no way I was going to make it upstairs to the bathroom. No way. I ran, clutching my stomach, down the hall, towards the front door, barging through even more bodies. I prayed the door wouldn't be locked. Oh please, God, don't let it be locked! I had images of barfing through the letter box running around in my head. A mass of whooping drunkards from the dining room chased me as I ran.

The door wasn't locked (thank you, God!). I ripped it open. A cool breeze was sharp against my sweaty face. I fell quickly to my knees as my stomach kicked and the taste of the chicken done in bread-crumbs I'd had for my tea, Thunderbird and somebody else's Southern Comfort hit me in reverse order.

A huge cheer went up from the crowd who'd followed me this far. They were slapping me on the back, clapping, hollering and laughing. I was leaning forward on my hands, shaking, perched halfway across the threshold. I closed my eyes. I wanted to die.

How did I feel? I'm sure you can guess.

Self-pity? Damn right. Oozing from every pore. And of course I blamed somebody else's Southern Comfort.

I was curled up on the bathroom floor, my eyes closed. I felt as if I was falling. I felt as if the world was tipping away beneath me and I was so heavy that I couldn't help myself from falling with it, head over heels, spinning backwards, over and over.

I tried to console myself that maybe things weren't quite as bad as I was making them out to be. After all, I wasn't the only one at the party who'd puked, the bathtub was evidence of that. Admittedly I seemed to be the only one who'd done it in front of everyone else, but did it really matter? Well, did it? I mean, you lived, you died, the world kept turning. I was only going to be jeered at and taunted for the rest of my life. And life never really amounted to much until it was over anyway, did it?

I let out a little sob and lay still.

I tried to think of happy things. Like Christmas. And the girl with the Gameboy. She was beautiful. She was something to be happy about, too. Or at least she would have been if I'd had the guts to talk to her, if I hadn't chundered on the doorstep in front of everybody. Oh God, had she seen me too? Had she been in amongst the crowd?

I gave up thinking of happy things, deciding to let myself drown in self-pity for a little while longer. It seemed easier.

I'm not sure how long it was that I lay foetal on that bathroom floor, but when the door was slammed into my back it shocked me out of drowsiness. Then when it hit me again, harder, I told whoever it was trying to get in to hold their horses for God's sake. At least the sharp pain along my battered spine dulled the queasy pain of my stomach.

I crawled to sit with my back against the bath, giving room to whoever wanted to get in. I didn't want to look at them. I took my glasses off and held my head down. Unfortunately I recognised the cherry-red Docs and the jeans with the hole in the knee.

'I'm sorry,' the girl with the Gameboy said. 'I didn't realise anybody was in here.' I could feel her staring at me and I tried to shrink a little. 'Are you okay?' she asked.

I forced myself to look up at her. She did look concerned to tell the truth. There was a brief wrinkle across her brow, a kind of sympathetic frown. She leaned forward and looked into the bathtub. I shook my head quickly. 'Wasn't me,' I told her. She turned her gaze to the toilet. I cringed. 'Sorry.'

'That's all right. Don't worry about it.' She lowered the lid and pulled on the flush. She sat herself down on the closed loo seat and stared at me. 'You look dreadful,' she said.

'Cheers.'

She giggled. She waved a hand in front of her mouth, trying to waft her laughter aside. 'I'm sorry, I know how you feel, honestly I do. I've been there plenty of times myself. It's just . . .' She giggled again. 'It's just I've never looked *quite* so bad as you.'

I shrugged. Well, what else could I do? I wanted to drown myself in the bath I was leaning on.

'I'm sorry,' she said again. 'I don't mean to be nasty, really I don't.'

She was smiling at me. I tried to smile back at her, but it was too lopsided, too embarrassed, so I let it fall away. It was no match for hers anyway. She had a smile that sparkled, and her eyes did too. They suddenly reminded me of a cartoon character's, a Tiny Toon or something. They seemed too clear and perfect to be real. So huge and so round, blue, with long, long lashes. They were like a baby's eyes. Even her nose sparkled, pierced with a tiny, jewelled stud that caught the light. She looked older than me, maybe twenty, twenty-one. She tucked her hair behind her ears. It was the same colour and shone just like the fur on my grandma's cat, Goldie. And I bet it was just as soft too.

Yes, I thought. Yes, I could fall in love, right here, right now. If I didn't have these lumpy bits of vomit trapped in between my teeth. If I didn't look and feel like shit on a shelf. And if this flaxen-haired beauty was able to see through this woeful exterior to the wonderous depths within. I offered her another lopsided smile in the hope . . . but she started laughing at me again.

'Oh, I'm sorry,' she said. She made an obvious effort to stifle her giggles, her hand wafting again. But it didn't work. Her giggles grew into guffaws, she started wiping at her eyes as the tears came, and even started bouncing up and down on her seat as the laughter rolled.

I sat there watching her, not believing what was happening to me. I'd really out-shamed myself this time.

'I'm really sorry,' she said, as best as she could, trying to draw enough breath for both laughter and words. 'I know you're desperately ill and everything, but I'm going to have to ask you to leave. I really need to go. I swear I'm going to wet myself in a minute.' And this seemed to make her laugh even more, her bouncing up and down becoming more frantic. 'Oh God, oh God. I'm sorry. Please. I can't . . .' She was on her feet now, dancing and jigging on the spot.

I stood up carefully, using the towel rail on the wall, a hand on my groaning stomach. I pushed myself off the bath, propelling my tortured body towards the door. I wanted to somehow apologise to this girl, but I had no idea what on earth I'd say. And anyway she was already lifting the toilet seat with one hand and fighting with the button on her jeans with the other, jigging around crazily all the time. So I left the room in silence, my head hung low. I closed the door behind me and stepped across the landing to sit on the top step of the stairs. I'd wait until she'd gone then sneak back into the bathroom, fill the bath to over-flowing and . . .

'There you are. I've been looking for you all over.' It was Paul, heading towards me, pushing through a couple of people sitting at the bottom of the stairs. His hair had been pulled out of its ponytail and hung straggly down his neck. 'Where've you been?'

I nodded at the bathroom door behind me. 'In there. Suffering.'

'I heard you'd puked,' he said. 'On the doorstep. You filled three milk bottles, you know?'

'Great.'

He was standing four or five steps below me, but we were face to face. I could see a smile beginning to creep across his.

I shook my head. 'Don't start,' I warned him.

But Paul couldn't help it. He began to chuckle quietly. 'Oh man, what've they done to you?'

'What d'you mean?' I asked suspiciously.

'Don't you know? Haven't you looked in a mirror?'

My friend's grin caused dread to spread like frost, cold and spikey, within me. I put my head in my hands. I thought I was going to cry. 'Oh God, Paul. What have they done to me?'

He took my fragile hand in his and led me like a child into the parents' bedroom. He switched on the light and stood me in front of the dressing table. He stood me right in front of the oval, pine-framed mirror. I looked at myself. I had no eyebrows. I closed my eyes and very slowly sat down on the edge of the bed.

'I'm sorry, mate,' Paul was saying. 'I didn't know they'd done it. I was up here with Jane Lois-Lane. I couldn't stop them.'

I felt completely drained of energy, bled dry. Unable even to get angry. I kept on thinking about the girl with the Gameboy. I kept thinking about how ridiculous I must have looked trying to give her a winning smile with no eyebrows. At least Paul had stopped laughing, it was just a pity he couldn't get rid of that smirk. But I forgave him. Maybe it was funny. And maybe one day I'd be able to laugh about it too. Just not in this century.

'Who?'

'That Laura lass I think.'

'Cow.'

'Yeah.'

I let out a huge sigh. 'I'm going home, Paul.' I was on my feet and heading for the door, avoiding the mirror.

He nodded. 'Yeah, okay. I'll come with you.'

'You don't have to. Stay with Jane Lois-Lane if you like.'

'Nar, it's okay. I'll see her some other time,' he said as we stepped out onto the landing. He pulled the door to behind us.

'Steady Progress?' I asked.

'I'd prefer to think of it as being rather rapid,' he grinned.

'Her boyfriend'll kill you.'

'Only if he catches me.'

I glanced at the bathroom door and could hear the sound of the flush going. I walked a little bit quicker. 'She won't mind you leaving will she?'

'Don't care if she does. I can't let my mate walk himself home when he's feeling ill now, can I? I've got to make sure he gets back all safe and sound. Can't have him falling in some gutter somewhere. He could get murdered or anything.'

'Wow, you're such a considerate person.'

'Sure am.'

'I never knew you cared so much.'

'Always have, always will. And don't you forget it.' He threw an arm around my shoulder as we made our way downstairs. 'I just wish you'd stop making such a sap of yourself whenever I take you anywhere. I've got a reputation you know.'

'I'm sorry.' I hated him for making me grin again. No matter how briefly.

Chapter Two

Paul had had really bright blond hair back then; Milky Bar Kid stuff. I met him when I first moved to Cleeston Comprehensive at the start of Year Eight. My parents had forced me to move, but I reckoned it was my brother's fault really. He'd made a complete hash of his GCSEs at Stonner Secondary School and even though my mum and dad had always known Robert was lazy, they'd also decided that the school should share some of the blame too. My father had realised quite early on that he could get both Robert and myself to do whatever he wanted as long as he shouted and cursed loud enough, and therefore claimed that any school not willing to shout and curse loudly simply wasn't the school for his children. So I'd found myself cycling the three miles into Cleeston Town every morning to get myself a better education.

The comp was an old school, built well over seventy years ago, and was quite a marked change to the modern Stonner Secondary. The corridors and classrooms seemed very dim and gloomy by comparison; the lights were too far up on the high ceilings to shed much light on a little thirteen-year-old like me. My new form room had been the art room and it was right at the far end of the school, the longest walk from anywhere else, down the dimmest corridor of all. But at least the toilets had only been next door.

Mrs Hobson, an old, frumpy maths teacher who hated giving As, and the Head of Year Eight had taken me to meet my new form on that first morning. She'd told me about another new boy, Justin from Bristol, who'd started at the comp at the end of the previous year, and she'd been going on and on about how wonderful it would be for the two of us to share our experiences of a new school together. I can remember not being at all sure whether to believe her or not; teachers and pupils often have contradictory ideas of what something *wonderful* entails.

Anyway, she'd walked into the room first and I'd tried to sneak in quietly behind her. But everybody had seen me. There had to have been near enough thirty alien faces all staring at me, weighing me up, deciding there and then whether or not to let me into their gang. I'd tried not to look too flustered or awkward, but I don't think it worked. My mum's fault this time, though.

I was all new to start at my new school, you see. New parka cagoule, new Clarks shoes with buckles instead of laces, new school uniform, new for-the-first-time-not-National-Health glasses and of course my new school bag containing my new pens, pencils, ruler, calculator etc. My mother had said she wanted me to make a good impression, but I've always reckoned it was really her who was trying to make the good impression.

So there I was; feeling uptight, looking uptight and being stared at by more than two dozen hostile faces. Mrs Hobson had tried to introduce me to my new form teacher, Miss Travis (a young and pretty English teacher who loved giving As), but I'd been too busy being stared at to listen. Then she'd introduced me to the form.

'2TR,' she'd said in that querulous voice of hers. 'I would like you to meet Christopher Ganin . . .'

I'd scanned the strange faces in front of me. I'd been desperate to find one who might seem friendly enough to sit with. I'd come up blank.

' . . . He's moved here from Stonner Secondary School and will be with most of you during your lesson time as well as registration . . .'

I'd gone to push my glasses up my nose (a habit of mine) but had suddenly realised I wasn't wearing them. They'd been tucked away in their new case at the bottom of my new bag because I hadn't wanted to be wearing them the first time people saw me. My mum hadn't been the only one trying to make a good impression, I suppose.

'He's looking forward to meeting all of you . . .'

In retrospect, I guess that bit was a lie.

' . . . and I'm sure you'll all make him feel very welcome.'

And I think that bit could have been a veiled threat.

Mrs Hobson had turned to me then. 'Right, Christopher. I'll leave you in the capable hands of Miss Travis. Don't forget you're always welcome to come and see me if you have any problems.' And with that she'd abandoned me, disappearing to more pressing Head of Year Eight duties elsewhere.

Miss Travis had told me it was a pleasure to have me in her form (I think she'd meant it, too) and had then said: 'Now, would you like to find a seat and I'll take the register.'

And with that all the eyes had suddenly dropped, all the heads had instantly turned. No one had wanted the new kid sitting next to them. I'd carried my new bag in between the big wooden tables and I'd never felt so alone or so vulnerable in the whole of my life. Everybody had been watching me, and yet nobody had actually been looking at me in case I'd managed to snag on to their stare and haul myself towards them. I'd turned to Miss Travis for help, but she'd been too busy shuffling the pages of her register to notice my distress. I'd wandered like a lost soul in search of rest among the paint splattered tables of the art room, but then a small, squeaky voice had come to my rescue.

Somebody at the back of the room had started waving their hand in the air and was shouting, 'Sit here. You can sit here if you want.' And at first I'd been extremely grateful to that wavy hand and squeaky voice, but as I'd pushed my way in between the tables towards it I'd realised the rest of the kids had started sniggering. And when I saw the owner of the hand and voice I understood why.

Which I realise must sound pretty nasty, but you've got to understand, the kid really *was* a gawk. (I say 'was' because he might not be now, and might some day read this.) He'd been wearing a horrible navy blue, auntie-knitted tank top, and his tie had had the fattest knot I'd ever seen. His strangely oval head had been sitting awkwardly lopsided on top of his long neck, and his hair had had one of those fake partings – the kind that only last five minutes after your mother has combed it into place, but you still spend the rest of the day pushing your fringe across your forehead anyway. I'd instantly realised that this was the class gawk offering me a seat at his lonely table, and had also instantly realised that this was Justin from Bristol whom Mrs Hobson had been trying to pair me off with. And the realisation had been truly frightening.

I'd walked all the way through the tables, pushing past the other sniggering kids, my new parka brushing their backs. I'd gone to Justin's table, but I hadn't sat down. I'd taken one of the stools from next to the boy without even looking at him and had carried it all the way back down to the front of the class. People had started laughing loudly then. I hadn't been able to see the look on Justin's face so I hadn't been sure whether it was aimed at me or at him, but I'd placed my stool in the aisle next to the desk where some lad with bright blond hair had been sitting.

Miss Travis had frowned at me. 'That's enough, class,' she'd said. She'd scowled down at me. 'Er, Christopher . . .?'

But I'd had a lie already prepared. 'Sorry, Miss, I've forgotten my glasses,' I'd said. I think I may have blushed because of the lie, but it had only succeeded in adding to the authenticity of my apparent blunder. 'I'll have to sit close to the blackboard so I can see properly, Miss,' I'd told her.

'Oh.' I can remember she'd seemed a little put out. 'Well all right then,' she'd said. 'But we'll have to find you a proper place for tomorrow.' And with a little bit of an embarrassed glance at Justin she'd returned to her desk and her big, blue registration book.

And I did feel bad for Justin, honest I did. It was just that I'd known how infectious gawkdom could be and I'd been worried that if my first friend at the comp had been a gawk then he could also have ended up being my last friend too.

Anyway, as it turned out I'd actually planted my chair next to Paul. And the first thing he ever said to me was: 'Bet you haven't really forgotten your glasses. Bet you just didn't want to sit next to my mate, Justin. I'm gonna beat you up at dinner.'

I remember it as if it were yesterday.

Obviously I'd tried to avoid Paul Stewart and his mates that first dinner time – he'd been a good couple of inches taller than me even then. I'd spent ages in the canteen even though I'd brought a packed lunch – I think I'd made each and every cheese and brown sauce sandwich last something like ten minutes or so. But eventually I'd had to leave and Paul, Ronnie Hickson and Liam Rothery had cornered me on the way to hide behind some big hardback reference book or other in the library.

The three of them had been waiting for me and as soon as I'd stepped out of the canteen door they'd appeared from behind one of those huge, metal wheelie bins. Paul had been wearing a pair of gold-framed glasses, and I can remember thinking that even with them on he was still much too lanky to really look like the Milky Bar Kid, before it had actually clicked that the glasses were mine.

I'd been as nervous as hell. 'Where'd you get them?' I'd said. 'Give them back.'

Paul had been as cocky as ever. 'Found them in your bag. You shouldn't go leaving your stuff around, you know,' he'd told me.

'Come on, give them back.' I'd been more scared he'd sprag me up to Miss Travis than of his promise to beat me up at that point.

'Thought you said you'd forgotten them.'

'Thought I had.'

'Good job I found them then, isn't it?' he'd said.

I just hadn't been able to believe it, my first day and already I was either going to get myself beaten up or grassed up, one or the other. I was clenching and unclenching my fists, and had started taking little steps backwards ready to dodge that throw of a punch I'd been so much expecting.

But then Paul had said, 'Lucky we hate Justin more than you. Want a game of tiggy?'

I'd simply stared at him.

He'd suddenly whipped my glasses off his face and handed them to me. 'Come on. We'll have a game of tiggy slapheads. You know how to play tiggy slapheads, don't you?'

I hadn't been able to say a word. I'd looked down at my new glasses in my hand, then back up at the face of this blond mop-topped kid who I could have sworn was going to smack me one.

'Foggy not It!' Liam had shouted.

'Foggy not It!' Ronnie and Paul had shouted simultaneously.

24

'Looks like you're It, Stonner. Give us twenty,' Paul had said and then run off with the other two in tow.

And at first I'd played their game with them simply because I'd felt that I ought to. It had seemed like the safest thing to do at the time. I hadn't been able to work this Paul character out. Had I passed some sort of initiation with him by slighting Justin from Bristol? Had the threat been simply that, a threat?

But it had been a good game. Tiggy slapheads was Paul's invention, a subtle variation on the usual game of tiggy. He'd had to explain the rules to me after I'd been running about hopelessly for at least ten minutes or so. He'd said:

'You can't tig like that, that's the whole point. You can't tig me normally. You've got to smack me on the back of the neck,' (and he'd made a cracking half-pistol, half-slapping noise) 'like that. But it's got to be hard enough to leave a mark you can see for the other person to be It.'

And that had been Paul all over. Never satisfied with normal ideas or games. He always got bored too quickly, too easily and too often with anything he'd deemed remotely ordinary. He even made up his own words. Or would rather replace certain words with a sound or facial expression (or both) which he thought described what he was trying to say a lot better than the original word did. As he got older this became more of a habit than anything else, and a bit of a joke too.

He'd loved tiggy slapheads in particular. He'd excelled in it. We'd played for the rest of the dinner time, non-stop, and not once did I manage to tig him. But he sure as hell managed to tig me. I have to admit that I'd chickened out a bit though and had gone mostly for Ronnie Hickson, the fat kid who hadn't been able to run so fast. But tiggy slapheads was a tactical game as much as it was a spiteful one. There was a lot of sneaking up on each other to be done if you were to land a decent blow. Of course, on the whole these guys had been better than me, but only because it had been my first game. And apart from being exhausted throughout most of that afternoon's lessons, I'd also squirmed in pain every time my collar had rubbed against that stinging sore patch of skin on the back of my neck.

My mother had cooked me my favourite meal for tea that night as a kind of treat; chicken done in breadcrumbs. She'd been pleased I'd made some friends. Of course I never told her the full story. She'd said that some people found it difficult fitting in to new situations. Without realising it she'd almost made me feel guilty about Justin. But probably not guilty enough, because the very next day I'd been sitting beside Paul on his table with Ronnie and Liam. Justin had stayed on his own at the back of the class.

Chapter Three

'Do they look *really* bad? I mean, are they *dead* obvious?'

Paul nodded. I appreciated the fact that he was at least *trying* not to laugh.

'Maybe I could get a pair of shades. They'd hide them, wouldn't they? What d'you reckon? Maybe? If I got big ones?'

Paul shrugged. 'Maybe.'

The night was warm and clear. We were sitting on a bench just inside the gates of the park at the bottom of Wollston Hill. The duck pond was dark before us, the ducks murmuring and grumbling at each other among the spilled feathers that littered the little rockery island in the middle. There was no wind, no breeze at all, and the water looked almost shiny solid.

'I can't believe I let them do it to me,' I groaned. 'That Laura's such a cow. She should have "cow" written on her T-shirt, not "babe".'

It was not quite midnight. We'd been sitting here for at least ten minutes. We'd been walking home from the party back to Paul's house (I was staying with him tonight so that I didn't have to get a taxi all the way back to Stonner), but we'd only made it this far. It was my fault. I'd been scared I was going to puke again. He only lived on the other side of the park, his house backed onto the football pitch, but my stomach just wasn't happy at all. It was burping and burbling away to itself, threatening to heave at any moment. My head wasn't much better; it felt as if it had been stuffed with thick cushions, and the world around me seemed somehow spongy, soft to the touch. My eyes weren't too hot either when I thought about it. I couldn't focus on anything without it slip-sliding away. In short, I was wrecked.

'How're you feeling?'

'Not so good,' I admitted. I watched the litter bin at my side casually slide out of view towards my left. The world just didn't seem stable anymore. 'Is it always like this?'

'What's that?'

'Does it always feel like this when you're a little bit drunk?'

Paul thought about it for a moment. 'It always feels like this when you're completely wrecked, yes. When you're a little bit drunk it feels slightly different. Not quite so bad.'

'It's my first time,' I told him.

'I know.'

I watched the litter bin glide smoothly away again. Then it suddenly occurred to me. 'How come you're not as bad as I am? You had as much as I did. How come I'm the only one spewing my guts up here?'

'I didn't have as much as you,' Paul told me. 'Nowhere near.'

'Yes, you did.'

He shook his head. 'You had at least three-quarters of that Southern Comfort you nicked . . .'

'Found.'

'Nicked.'

I ignored him. 'But you were on the cider with Jane Lois-Lane . . .'

'I only had a couple of mouthfuls.'

'What happened anyway?'

Paul frowned. 'Eh?'

'You know. With you and Jane Lois-Lane? You didn't, you know, did you?'

'Don't be soft,' he said angrily. 'What d'you take me for?'

Some people may have thought it was to Paul's credit that he was still a virgin, they may have claimed it was quite sensible, moral even, in one so young. Of course, they'd be completely wrong. In Paul's eyes you see, he'd just never been able to find anybody he thought was good enough to give his virginity to.

'She's nice,' he told me. 'But not that nice.'

And I nodded in an understanding kind of way. But deep down I was wishing that my reasons why not were also due to choice.

'So, tell me what happened then.'

He winked at me. 'The trousers worked perfectly,' he said pinching at the thighs of his Magical Pulling Pants. 'They never fail. I've not met a woman yet who can resist them.'

'Did she say anything about her boyfriend?'

'Not a word,' he said. 'Not a word.' He stood up, and let a huge grin slither its way across his face. He opened his arms wide and looked up at the stars. 'Oh man, she's . . .' (he gave a long, low wolf whistle).

I grinned back at him. 'And . . .?'

'I tell you,' he beamed at me. 'You should have been there. Well, no, I guess you shouldn't have. But you know what I mean.' He gave me a little mime as he talked, lots of hand gestures, pacing up and down in front of the dark pond. 'I made a bit of Steady Progress with her downstairs, you know? I think you were still in the land of the living at that point, underneath the table . . .'

I nodded, still grinning like a loon.

'We did a bit of kissing. Lips first, moving slowly onto her neck. She's a great kisser. I held her hand. We did a bit more,' (he made slurpy kissing noises). 'But hey, I didn't push anything too far, you know? I was the perfect gentleman, and don't you forget it.'

I shook my head. I wouldn't dare.

'I told her how beautiful she was looking, told her how I'd always fancied her, 'cos women go for that kind of thing, don't they? And it was her that first mentioned going upstairs.'

'Straight up?'

'Straight up. She just turned round and said (he put on a pretty good impression of the girl), ' "Paul? Don't you think we should go somewhere a bit more private?" '

'And what did you say?'

'Whey-hey-hey! That's what I said. So we left you under the table, you were snoring pretty well by that point, and I led her upstairs to Matty's sister's room. She had her hands *all* over me, kept on feeling my backside as we walked . . .'

'I didn't know Matty had a sister.'

'Oh, yeah, sorry, I forgot to tell you. You know the girl with the Gameboy? Yeah? Well, that's Matty's sister, Katie. She never went to the comp. She went to that all girls' school near Mayborough.'

'Wow,' I said. And Paul raised his eyebrows with me, because the pair of us had always had a thing about that school near Mayborough. 'How old is she?'

'Nineteen. She's at uni now. She's doing art, painting and stuff.'

I nodded. 'I thought she seemed older than us.'

Paul waited for me to look at him. 'So me and Jane Lois-Lane were in Matty's sister's room and . . .'

'She's dead gorgeous you know.'

'Who?'

'Katie.' I looked at him. 'The girl with the Gameboy. Matty's sister.'

'Not bad I suppose. But anyway, Jane was wearing this dead lacey . . .'

'And I made a complete sap of myself in front of her.' I put my head in my hands. 'There I was, puking up in the bathroom . . . And d'you know what I said to her?'

Paul shook his head. 'No. What?'

I shook mine. 'I've forgotten. But it was probably something really stupid.'

'Probably.'

'And I didn't even have any eyebrows,' I sobbed.

Paul came and sat back down next to me. He put an arm around my shoulder. 'Don't worry, mate. They'll grow back in a couple of weeks. Just buy some shades and pray for sunny weather.'

'Great.'

I got unsteadily to my feet and started walking away. Paul followed. We skirted around the blackly shining duck pond, and weaved in between the steel frames of the swings in the kiddies' play area.

'What you need is cheering up,' Paul told me.

I humfed back at him, my head down, watching my feet. We clambered over a low, wooden fence and headed out across the flat, lifeless footy pitch.

'Me and Jane Lois-Lane were talking . . .'

'Was that before or after you should've been protecting me from nasty cows with razors?' I asked.

'Shut up a minute and listen, will you?'

'Sorry.'

'Right. Anyway, we were talking about going away to university and that. And she was asking me where I was going and what degree I was going to do.'

'You're not, though. You said you were staying here to get a job.'

'I know, that's what I told her.'

'I'm going. I'm going to do English at Newcastle.'

'Yeah. I told her that too.'

'And maybe I'll find some proper friends who won't be too busy snogging when I need them to defend my eyebrows.'

Paul stopped walking. 'Look, d'you wanna know what she said or what?'

'Sorry.'

'Okay.' He took a deep breath and started walking again. 'She said that it would be really strange, me and you splitting up. She reckoned it'd be like an end of an era thing. You know, Cleeston wouldn't be the same without Paul and Chris . . .'

'Chris and Paul.'

'Yeah. Right. Anyway, she said that she'd never really seen Paul without Chris. Or Chris without Paul. She reckoned that when she'd first moved to our school she'd thought we were brothers or something.'

That made me smile.

'So, I was thinking . . . Are you listening?'

I nodded.

'So, I was thinking that maybe we ought to do something a bit special, you know? Significant. Seeing as it is the end of an era and everything. Do something that'd really seal the friendship.'

'I'm not going to sleep with you, Paul.'

He laughed. 'Good job. I've seen your legs, it'd be like doing it with a gibbon.'

'So, what brilliant idea did you come up with this time, then?'

We'd both stopped walking. We were standing slap-bang on the battered and off-white centre spot, the pitch was dark and silent around us. The whole park was empty of people apart from Paul and me.

'It was you who gave me the idea actually,' Paul said. 'When you were going on about Matty's living room being all red and you thought you were swimming through your own blood.'

'I was a corpuscle.'

'Yeah, whatever. Anyway, that's what gave me the idea.' He grinned at me hugely. 'We could become blood brothers.' He didn't wait for me to answer. 'You know, like the Red Indians used to do? Cut each other's hand and become brothers instead of just friends. Become more than friends. It'd be really cool. Blood on blood, like in that Bon Jovi song.'

'I don't like Bon Jovi.'

'You like that song though, don't you?'

'Never heard it.'

'I'll play it for you, it's great, you'll love it.' He watched my face carefully, peering at me in the dark. 'So what d'you reckon? Are you up for it?'

To tell the truth, it did sound like a pretty good idea to me. It sounded kind of . . . adventurous. I nodded. A smile began to grow. 'Yeah. Yeah, okay then,' I said. 'I've shared everything else with you. I guess a little blood won't matter.'

Paul started laughing. 'I knew you'd do it,' he said. 'I knew you'd think it was cool.' He began walking quickly away, heading towards the fence at the bottom of his garden. 'Come on,' he called. 'We'll do it now. We'll do it in the bathroom.'

I groaned. I should have known this was coming. 'Oh no, not tonight, Paul. I feel as rough as hell. I don't think my stomach can take the sight of blood as well. Can't we wait until the morning? Come on, we'll do it in the morning, okay?'

'Don't be such a wuss,' he shouted back. He was almost sprinting away now. 'If we do it tonight I'll be able to nick one of my dad's razor blades.'

'Razor blades? You never mentioned razor blades!'

'How else are we supposed to cut our hands?' He stopped and turned round to look at me. 'And anyway, it's good you're drunk, 'cos then the pain won't be as bad, will it? I'm the one who should be worrying.'

I groaned. I didn't believe him.

'Sure you wanna do this?'

'Are you?'

'I asked you first.'

'So?'

'So nothing. Look, I'm not going to mess about. Either we do it or we don't, okay?'

'Okay.'

'I don't want you giving me any hassle. It's gonna be, you know,' he sucked hard and sharp through his teeth giving a pained expression, 'we both know that. So you'd better say something now if you reckon we'd better just forget all about it. I don't care, it's up to you. If you want to do it, then we do it. If you don't, we don't. All right?'

'All right.'

'You were all for it a couple of minutes ago. You couldn't wait to do it, remember? So you'd better decide what you really want. And stop giving me all this hassle. We do it or we don't. Okay?'

'Okay.'

'So do you wanna do it, or don't you?'

'Do you?'

Paul glared at me. I shrugged. He was about to say something else, something nasty too by the look on his face, but movement from his parents' bedroom restrained him. I caught myself hoping our argument had woken his dad up, got him out of bed, and would bring him through to the bathroom to ask just what the hell we thought we were doing with one of his razor blades at this time of night?

We waited silently but no one came to disturb us.

We both looked at the blade.

Paul was holding it tentatively between his thumb and forefinger. He held it once more under the rush of cold water from the tap. It simply shrugged the water off. It was hard, tough. I looked at my hand. It was trembling.

Paul was staring at me. I had the horrible feeling I was going to be trapped in this room with him until I let him slice my hand up with that razor blade. For all his words about it being my decision I could tell that he'd already made up his mind, and that was what mattered to him. He'd keep me locked up and chained here until I agreed to go ahead with it.

It was the pain I was worried about. I really wanted to become blood brothers, I thought it was a brilliant idea, one of Paul's best. I just knew it was going to hurt. That was the problem. When I was younger I'd always wanted a tattoo, I'd always thought they were pretty cool, and I'd promised myself that I'd get one as soon as I was eighteen. But my eighteenth birthday had come and gone several months ago and I still didn't have one. I'd told everybody it was because I hadn't found the right design yet, which was kind of true. The fact that I was scared it would hurt I guess was slightly truer. But please don't think I'm a chicken or a wuss or anything, it's just that I've always been allergic to pain, that's all.

We both looked at the blade.

It winked ominously in the artificial light. The window blind was up and the blackness of the night outside reflected the scene inside on the patterned glass of the window like a fuzzy mirror. Translucent, my memory curiously wanted to tell me. That was what that patterned glass effect was called. My hand was opaque though. So was the blade. Was blood opaque? I couldn't remember ever wanting to know before. Or was it translucent? It certainly wouldn't be transparent. It would look stupid if you could see clearly through blood. Although maybe unhealthy blood was transparent . . .?

Paul was staring at me again. I tried to avoid his gaze but he wouldn't let me. He held the blade out to me, offering me the chance to cut him first. I moved to say something but he shook his head, gesturing in the general direction of his parents' bedroom. He didn't want me to speak, he didn't want them woken. He offered me the blade again, more forcefully, thrusting it under my nose. And I took it. Carefully. It was all right for him, at least he could think straight. I was still desperately trying to climb out of my spongy pit of alcoholic stupor.

But someone had greased the sides. And I blamed the git who'd bought the Southern Comfort. I reckoned he could have at least hidden it somewhere more original. If I wanted to hide my drink I would have thought of a much better place to hide it, everybody hid their bottles in the washing machine. Or the microwave. If I was hiding something I'd have put it . . .

Paul held his hand out towards me. Right hand, palm up. I pushed my glasses up my nose. I took hold of his wrist. I gritted my teeth. It was now or never. If I really wanted to do this then I had to do it now.

We both looked at the blade.

The house was completely silent around us. I held Paul's hand over the deep-blue washbasin and gripped the razor blade as tightly as I could between my sweaty fingers. I blinked hard, one final attempt to clear my head. And it worked. Kind of. But my hand wouldn't stop trembling. I was frightened of hurting him. For all his bravery I could feel his hand flicking and twitching against mine. He was biting on his bottom lip.

Holding the blade as steady as I could, forcing myself to concentrate on what I was doing, I touched the wafer-thin metal down against the palm of Paul's hand. He winced. He cringed. He hissed at me through his teeth. He left his hand in mine but tried to move the rest of his body as far away from me as possible. I never took my eyes away from the blade, one shiny corner disappearing deeper into the pink flesh. I could actually feel his skin slicing away beneath the blade, ridging against the lines on his palm. I ran the blade for over an inch across his hand. The blood seemed slow at first, but very thick and very dark. He held his hand over the basin. Big, red droplets exploded on the plastic surface.

He was breathing heavily, as if he'd just run a race. But he looked relaxed. Maybe it didn't hurt as much as he'd been expecting it to? Or maybe he was simply glad the cutting part was over for him now. He took the blade from me and held my hand as I'd held his. I wanted to close my eyes, but there was no way I could. They were fixed on the blade as intently as ever. I used my free hand to grip the arm of my glasses, holding them in place.

The pain was hot. It was a hot needle of pain buried deep into my hand. Paul drew the blade slowly, so slowly, along the line of the cut. I saw the blood come. I was kind of relieved, I was hoping it would cool the heat of the blade. I saw it well up and then flow. I was glad it looked healthy anyway, thick and opaque, not at all transparent. And it somehow felt like a contradiction to me. The blood was slow, gentle across my palm, but within my hand the hurt was sharp and intense.

Paul dropped the bloodied blade into the sink. It slipped down the blue plastic to chink against the plughole.

A silence stretched out between us. It was really beginning to feel kind of strange now, kind of special. The jokes, the taunts had all stopped. The blood had our full attention. Paul held up his hand as if to bless me. His blood ran down over his wrist and forearm, seeping into the cuff of his shirt.

'Blood brothers,' Paul said.

I nodded. I couldn't help grinning. I felt so good. So big and so strong.

'Blood brothers.'

We clasped each other's hand. My blood joined with Paul's to trickle down his wrist. We were becoming blood brothers. There were no flashing lights, no big trumpets in the background, just quiet. A low, absorbing silence as our wounds bled into each other. Our grip felt slimy, uncomfortable, a little bit painful, but we didn't let go. The patterned glass of the bathroom window mirrored us in the light as we stood there. I watched Paul. Paul watched our hands.

This was it. We were actually making something out of our friendship; something good, something special. In fact something a lot more special than either of us could ever have dreamed. Creation in the making.

'Look at the state of my bandage, it's soaked. I'm still bleeding.'

'Just as long as it's your blood you're wasting, not mine.'

'How am I going to explain this to my mum?'

'Tell her the truth.'

'I can't do that. She'll go mad.'

'What for? It's not as if you've done anything wrong.'

'She'd say I was stupid. She'd say it was a really stupid and childish thing to do. She just wouldn't get the point, you know? She'd go on about diseases and stuff.'

'Hey! Just what are you trying to say?'

'You did have a wash this morning, didn't you?'

'Of course I did.'

'That's all right then. She's got nothing to worry about, has she?'

PART TWO

Chapter Four

Bus surfing had been one of Paul's favourite pastimes when we were younger. Needless to say he'd soon got me involved and hooked on the sport. And although he'll never admit it, I reckon I was better at it too. Naturally well balanced, that was me.

Of course you had to choose the right bus, and we'd always found the 3C to be about the best. The 3C's route took the bus out of town towards Stonner (which was handy for me) and then on further into the countryside, calling at most of the surrounding villages in a big, lopsided circle before ending up just outside McDonald's on Market Street about three quarters of an hour later.

Although the length of the 3C's journey wasn't the only reason we liked to surf it. It was also the exact route it followed, from Stonner to Huxley to Cranidge to Mayborough and Worley. These had to be the most windy, twisting roads in the whole of the area. There were uphill and downhill curves, both left and right, a tight U-turn outside Huxley Post Office and even a humpbacked bridge on the way into Mayborough. Our poise, balance and endurance were tested to the highest

41

degree. We boarded the bus as boys, but came back bus surfing heroes.

It was us against the driver. We'd try to suss him (or, very rarely, her) as we boarded the bus and paid our fare. Did they have the close-set eyes of a speed-freak, the tight expression and clenched-teeth grimace we associated with impatient drivers? Or were they disappointingly too old or too nervous looking and twitchy even to get the double-decker out of second gear? We'd stare the driver in the eyes as we paid our 90p, psyche him out; let him know we could handle anything he could throw at us, that we weren't scared of his late breaking and clumsy gear changes. Then it was upstairs and to the back of the bus where we'd take our positions and ready ourselves for the corners, S-bends and tight downhill curves to come.

Other passengers could often be a problem; old women were usually the worst. They'd sit there in their tatty headscarfs, clutching their shopping bags, tutting and scowling at us. Some would even go so far as telling the driver, but only as they were getting off the bus. Other teenagers could be a pain too, and they weren't always quite so easy to ignore, but at least they'd never sprag on us to the driver. Probably too busy doing something they shouldn't have been doing themselves.

Anyway, we'd be standing in the narrow aisle between the seats, me behind Paul, our arms outstretched to either side, one foot in front of the other and slightly apart, knees bent (the knees were the crucial bit, you always had to remember to use your knees before your feet). The 3C would leave Stonner on the last solid straight before the road out of Worley in well over half an hour's time and Paul and I would let ourselves relax into the feel of the bus beneath our feet, bending our knees to loosen them up, twisting our waists, leaning forward and back as far as we could go to warm up the important muscles.

Then the first bend would hit us.

Left-hander, not too sharp, we knew it well. We'd compensate for the movement of the bus without too much difficulty. I'd be looking over Paul's shoulder, at the road coming towards us, watching for the second left-hander which would lead us into the downhill S-bend. Then we'd know the journey had *truly* begun.

And it's a lot more difficult than it sounds, especially on the 3C. By the end we'd be exhausted, but more often than not, triumphant too. In between times however, there'd be a lot of twisting and stumbling, a lot of windmilling of arms and banging of knees into hard, painful seats. And forty-five minutes seems like an age when you're pushing your body to its limit of physical endurance – ask any other true athlete. We only allowed ourselves to rest during the 3C's journey when the bus passed the all-girls school on the outskirts of Mayborough. We'd decided this would be the most strategic point to rest after we'd both several times suffered injuries by concentrating on the school rather than the surf.

We used to keep a record of our fastest times. I think I've still got the chart Paul made at the bottom of some drawer or other. We'd time the journey and then add twenty seconds for every fall or every time we had to grab hold of each other to stay upright. Our fastest ever was forty-one minutes and five seconds, and that included only one fall (we still argue over whose it was). There was one time when we could have gone even faster, maybe even broken the forty minute barrier, but Paul had gotten a bit excited and cocky, like he does. Although, as it turned out, it wasn't really the surf that was the important part.

It was during the Easter holidays in that first year I spent at the comp. We were the only passengers on the bus and the driver had been speeding along even though it was pouring. Neither of us had fallen yet and I'd been really excited by how well we were doing. We'd barely been able to see out through the windows in front of us, but were surfing the bends with ease, and we'd ridden the U-turn outside Huxley Post Office with what could only be described as pure finesse. We'd taken our brief rest at the usual point, frustrated because of the misted-up windows, and the only big obstacle left to conquer had been the humpbacked bridge on the way into Mayborough. It was then Paul had turned to me and called over his shoulder, 'You feeling lucky?'

Admittedly I could have said no and been able to keep on my feet, and then we would have probably broken that elusive forty minute barrier, but I suppose I'd been feeling pretty full of myself too.

'The bridge,' he'd shouted. 'D'you reckon you could hang-five over the bridge?'

'Do you?'

'No sweat.'

'Anything you can do, I can do twice,' I'd told him.

And he'd replied, 'In your dreams, Stonner.' (It had taken him at least another year before he'd started calling me Chris.)

We'd squinted through the misty windows and rain, and had just been able to make out the narrow bridge ahead. The bus had dipped down a hill, shallow curves in the road brought it in and out of view from behind the trees. It had always been one of the trickiest of obstacles anyway, it was so difficult to move with the bounce of the bus's suspension, but we'd known that surfing it on one foot was going to be a real killer.

We'd felt the bus slow down, the driver negotiating the last bend before the bridge. We'd negotiated that last bend too. Then he'd accelerated slightly. True to form this particular driver had kept his speed above the norm. The bridge had come closer and closer. I can remember thinking that the hump had surely grown since the last time I'd seen it. Then:

'Now!' Paul had shouted.

Instantly we'd both lifted a foot off the deck. The front wheels of the 3C had hit the bridge. We'd felt the suspension give, then bounce . . . And to cut a long story short we'd both ended up in a pile on the cold metal flooring.

As I remember we'd both been a little too bruised to continue the surf and so had simply let the bus carry us through Mayborough and towards Worley. We'd both been a bit disappointed at not breaking the forty minute barrier.

'Wouldn't it be cool if we could bus surf properly,' Paul had said. 'You know, if the driver would let us stand on the roof.'

I think I'd nodded, although deep down I'd thought it was a stupid idea.

'It'd be just like flying,' Paul had said. 'I wish I could fly. You know, like Superman. That'd be even cooler.'

'I had a dream once where I could fly,' I'd said (I still have them in fact). 'I don't think I was Superman though.'

'Oh, I wouldn't actually want to *be* Superman,' Paul had told me.

'So who would you be? If you could be any super hero, which one would you be?'

Paul had shrugged. 'Batman's the best, but he can't fly. I've got to be able to fly.' He'd been sitting with his head lightly bouncing against the glass of the window. It was the sort of question he really enjoyed thinking about. 'But I wouldn't want to be any of the super heroes that are around at the minute. They're all the same really, they just go round beating people up. I'd want to be a new one. I wouldn't want to be really strong, because then all you have to do is hit people all the time and that's dead boring. My super power would be with my mind. Instead of breaking their legs I'd screw them up in their heads, make them go insane. Make their brains dribble out of their ears.' He'd grinned massively at me.

I hadn't fully agreed with him. I'd always fancied the idea of being really strong. 'It'd still be cool to be good at fighting, though,' I'd said. 'Beat them up a bit *before* you fried their brain.'

'Yeah, but if your mind was your super power then you could move objects with it and drop pianos and cars and stuff on them anyway.' He'd whistled like the sound of a falling object, then made a noise that sounded something like 'kersplat' only messier. 'And you could read people's minds too. You could read Lisa Horner's mind and find out if she liked you or not.'

I'd laughed, in an embarrassed, guilty, nervous kind of way. Back then my feelings for Lisa Horner were a secret I wasn't too sure how much I trusted him with.

And Paul must have noticed my sudden awkwardness, because he'd then started to make me feel even worse. 'How many bad guys would you beat up to save Lisa Horner?' he'd teased. 'I bet you'd wear tights like Superman if Lisa Horner wanted you to.'

I'd tried to argue back, but all I'd been able to to say was, 'Get lost, as if I would.' But we'd both known it was a lie.

'I can just imagine it now,' he'd said, jumping out of his seat. 'Super Stonner to the rescue!' And he'd run up and down the bus pretending to beat up bad guys with all the sound effects at his disposal. 'Super Stonner to the rescue! Super Stonner to the rescue!'

I'd been really glad when the bus had finally pulled up outside McDonald's on Market Street and Paul at long last had had to get off. More and more people had been getting on the bus the closer it had come to town, and his voice had kept on rising in volume with each new passenger. He'd really made me squirm, in the way only best friends holding your darkest secret can. Not that it had ever stopped me from going bus surfing with him again, or had even spoiled the friendship any. Admittedly he'd gone on to completely humiliate me in front of Lisa Horner, but I'm sure I got my own back somewhere along the way.

And to tell the truth, I'd always thought that the way he'd called me Super Stonner was something of a compliment.

Chapter Five

I opened my eyes carefully. The curtains were still closed and the morning light was gentle. I opened them a bit wider, staring up at my bedroom ceiling. I reckoned my headache was up there somewhere, floating around near the lightshade, waiting to dive-bomb straight back down at me when I was least expecting it.

My bed was warm and soft, the room was still; I could hear my mother moving about downstairs. The headache had gone.

But I didn't trust it. I slid slowly out of bed and walked quietly around my bedroom, looking for it. Because I was sure it was out there, somewhere. Hiding. It was probably lurking in a corner, ready to pounce.

I'd been *so* ill after the party. And I hadn't thought it to be at all fair. My parents had of course blamed the drink. I'd received lectures from both of them on separate occasions, both telling me that I'd never seen them in such a state, both telling me they never wanted to see me in such a state ever again. I hadn't argued with them. I wish I had, but I hadn't had much strength to do anything at the time.

I couldn't believe that this was the way I was going to start my first days of freedom.

The stomach pains had lasted for all of Saturday morning and well into Saturday afternoon (I was only sick once more though). It had been the headache that had gone on and on. And on. It hadn't really felt like a normal headache either. Most headaches stick their needles in at the front, just behind your forehead, but this one had throbbed right at the back of my skull, deep inside, almost at the base of my brain. It had hurt so badly that even my thoughts were barbed.

It had taken my mother until Sunday night before she finally decided to feel some concern for me. Even she knew a hangover shouldn't last this long or have me feeling quite this bad. She was on tenterhooks anyway, because of my brother who was also laid-up in bed. He'd caught salmonella from eating dodgy eggs and was losing weight rapidly.

So with both of her sons praying for a quick death, my mother had decided to call the doctor in first thing yesterday morning to see me. But he was worse than useless. Every time he'd touched my head with those hot, stabbing fingers of his I'd felt like I was going to scream. He'd told my mum he couldn't find anything wrong with me and had then made some crack about youngsters not being able to handle their drink. He'd told me to leave alcohol to the professionals. So thanks to him my mother soon managed to lose all of her sympathy again.

And I'd laid in bed telling myself that one day, one day soon, I was going to get really drunk on whisky, go round to the good doctor's house, and piss through his letter box.

I peered at myself in the mirror on my wardrobe door. I looked all right. Fairly normal apart from the lack of eyebrows. I ran my fingers through my hair, tentatively probing at my scalp, still waiting for the headache. After suffering with it for three whole days I couldn't quite believe it had cleared up as quickly and easily as this. I'd fallen asleep last night feeling as though my pillow was made of broken glass, and I'd woken up this morning without even a sniff of pain. I placed my hands on either side of my head and gave it a good, hard squeeze. Nothing.

I smiled at myself in the mirror. And the mirror smiled back.

I did a little dance. I threw open the curtains and pushed wide the window to let some fresh air into the room. It was a glorious day outside. Now I could start my non-school days properly. I danced a bit more. I felt great. I boogied over to my wardrobe and searched through the pile at the bottom where I'd dumped the clothes my mum had just washed, and, still bopping away, flung a clean pair of jeans, T-shirt, socks and undies onto the bed behind me. I'd never felt so good. I felt absolutely brilliant.

Hit the road headache, and don't you come back no more.

I dressed, singing to myself. In my exuberance I'd scattered my clothes far and wide across my bedroom, my undies being the only item to actually land on the bed. I shimmied around the room singing to myself, picking them up and putting them on as I went. All except one of my socks. It had flown straight out of the window and, looking down, I could see it on the porch roof. I didn't care. It was one of those days.

I was already making plans for the day, and first on the list was a visit to Paul's house. My mum had told me that he'd been pretty ill over the past couple of days as well. So I'd go round to make sure he was okay, and if he was feeling any better we'd head into town and wander around the precinct watching all the good-looking lassies in their short summer skirts. Maybe even go for a pint or two.

I thought I heard my mum calling my name, and shouted that I'd be down as soon as I'd had a wash. Then I danced my way through into the bathroom. I'd hated the last three days, partly because I was ill, but mainly because they were days of freedom I was losing. But not today. No more wastage. The whole of summer lay before me now, waiting for Paul and me to show it a good time. I remembered that strange, uplifting feeling I'd felt when we'd become blood brothers and it came flooding back again. And I let it fill the bathroom much the same as the glorious sun had filled my bedroom. I wouldn't even let my eyebrowless reflection faze me.

My mother called again.

'Just a minute,' I shouted.

There was a dull throbbing in my bandaged hand. I guessed I must have knocked it when I'd been acting the fool, dancing around. I had to admit to being a little worried about it. My mother had wanted Dr Wheeler to look at it, but I wouldn't let him. No way was I going to have someone like him asking stupid questions.

My mother stuck her head around the bathroom door. 'Did you shout?' she asked.

'I just said I'd be down in a minute,' I told her. 'After you'd called up the second time.'

'I didn't call,' she said.

I shrugged. 'Sorry, I thought you had. You must have been talking to Robert or something.'

Mum shook her head. 'No, he's asleep. I was tidying up downstairs.' She came into the bathroom and put her hand against my forehead, feeling for a temperature. 'You seem a bit better today. You're not quite as pale this morning.'

'I feel fine. I got up this morning and the headache had gone and everything.'

My mother nodded, a slight frown appearing on her face. 'Good,' she said. Then: 'I just hope it teaches you a lesson. You even had your father talking about brain scans last night, he was that worried.' She shook her head at me. 'God help you if you ever come home in that kind of state again, young man. I won't be so sympathetic next time round.'

I wanted to tell her that I didn't think she'd been all that sympathetic this time round, but had enough wisdom to keep my mouth shut.

'I don't know what on earth my mother would have said if I'd ever come home in the kind of state you did on Saturday morning. I would have been out on my ear, no doubt. It's every time you and Paul get together, isn't it? You're both as stupid as each other. You do realise his mother's had the doctor to him twice?'

'But he hadn't been drinking that much.'

'He must have been. Don't take me for a fool. Anyway, you'd better give him a ring and see how he is. And I think you'd better apologise to his mother for being sick on her landing while you're at it, don't you?'

'I was planning on going round to see him anyway.'

'Well, I'm sorry but you'll just have to give him a ring instead. I'm going to see your Aunt Jenny and I need you to stay in and look after Robert.'

'But...'

'But nothing. You've had your father and me waiting on you hand and foot for the last three days, so you can just stay in and do me one favour today. All right?'

I would have argued if I'd thought it might have done any good. By the time my mother went out, approximately ten minutes later, she'd successfully managed to destroy my good mood, my optimism, and my reason for living. My summer was now a lump of ice floating on the sea, with me perched precariously on top, already scared of straying too near the edge for fear of slipping in. At first the ice had seemed huge, massive, a virtual glacier, but now it was drifting towards warmer waters. I could see it melting around me, dissolving away everywhere I looked.

I slumped in front of the telly. I didn't watch the programme. The light from the living room window was reflected on the screen and I could see myself reflected there as well. I ignored the daytime presenters and stared at my own petulant reflection instead.

What a horrible week. What a horrible summer. What a horrible life!

Robert called me. I sighed heavily, cursing under my breath, and headed upstairs. The pain in my hand had got worse. I must have banged it quite badly for it to be throbbing like this.

My brother's room was dark. It smelt of illness. I poked my head round the door and asked him what he wanted. He didn't reply. I took a breath, not wanting to breathe in any of his lurgy fumes and stepped into his room. He was a big, dark mass underneath his quilt. He looked as though he was asleep, and when I stepped closer still I could hear him gently snoring.

I could have sworn he'd called my name. But it didn't really bother me, at least I didn't have to do anything for him. I closed his bedroom door quietly as I left. And once more he called my name. But when I held my breath and looked inside again, he still hadn't moved. Was he taking the mick? I got up real close to him, even called his name quietly, but he seemed pretty much asleep to me. Over the years however, I've learned never to trust my older brother. So I punched him.

He jolted, suddenly awake. He stared up at me groggily, blinking his eyes. 'What . . .? What's wrong?' he asked, in his best feeble voice.

'Did you call?' I asked. 'Did you want something?'

He shook his head. 'No. I've been asleep.'

'Well, somebody called me,' I said.

He moved to sit up in bed, pushing the covers aside and the smell of somebody who'd been in bed for over a week moved with him. I remembered I wasn't holding my breath any more and stood up quickly, backing away. I had to admit that my brother did look poorly. He was ghostly pale in the darkness of his room, and not that he'd ever been fat, but his face was very long and thin, not at all how he used to look. He'd never had cheekbones before.

'Are you sure you didn't call me?'

'I said I was asleep, didn't I?'

I shrugged. 'Yeah, sorry.' I went to leave, but he said:

'While you're here, can you switch my telly on?'

I nodded and did as he asked.

'Can you put it on my desk where I can see it better?'

I sighed, but did it anyway.

'The picture's not very good,' he said.

So I fiddled with the aerial.

'And put it on BBC. I hate Richard and Judy.'

'Is there anything else I can do for you? You said you didn't want anything a minute ago.'

'Could you get me something to eat? Just some toast or something?'

I heaved a sigh loud enough for the neighbours to hear. 'Do you want scrambled eggs on that?' I hissed as I stalked out of the room, but I don't think he got the joke. I wished I'd punched him harder when I'd had the chance. I was sure I owed him a few from when I was younger anyway.

The two of us had never been close; we'd never really liked each other, or even tried to get on. He was bigger than me, older than me, stronger than me, and had always wanted to prove it (had probably enjoyed proving it, too). I'd been his personal stress reliever. If he'd had a bad day at school, if he'd got in trouble with the teachers, or had been rejected by Hannah Cockburn for the seven hundredth time that term, then he'd always been able to make himself feel happier by pinning me down and slapping me around a bit. Not that I'd taken all of it lying down of course. I was never able to beat him at his own physical-torture game, but now and again I'd manage to sprag him up for most of the things that went wrong at home, including most of the things that had been my fault really. I guess I'd just had a sweeter smile than Robert and therefore my parents had always believed me rather than him. So maybe the beatings had in actual fact just been his way of trying to wipe that sickening smile off my face.

I went downstairs. My hand was getting worse, the pain was nearly as bad as when Paul had cut me in the first place. That'd be just my luck, I thought as I popped a couple of rounds of bread in the toaster. Just my luck if I got gangrene or something. And of course, I'd blame Paul if I did.

Robert called me.

I tutted. 'Yeah, yeah. In a minute.'

– Chris –

I shouted: 'Come on. Give me a chance. I've only just put the bread in.' But I thought: Impatient git!

– Chris, can you hear me? –

'Look, for God's sake . . .' I stopped dead in my tracks. That wasn't Robert's voice.

Something like the cold, tickling legs of a spider ran along my spine. The voice wasn't coming from my brother's room. The voice hadn't even come from upstairs. I couldn't stop the involuntary shiver as the voice came again, calling my name. I looked around myself in the kitchen, but deep down I knew the owner of it wouldn't be there. I even looked out of the window and into the back garden knowing I wouldn't see him there either. Not hidden behind the shed, not even crouched in between the fence and the greenhouse. I felt as though I was simply going through the motions of what I thought I should do before I finally admitted that the voice was actually coming from inside my head.

I looked at my bandaged hand. It felt as though it had been plunged into a kettle of boiling water.

– Chris –

I was completely silent when I asked: – Paul? Is that you? –

I drove very slowly into Cleeston to Paul's house. Not because I'd taken the car without asking, but because I wasn't sure whether or not I really wanted to get there. I'd left Robert with his toast and begged him not to tell Mum and Dad that I was taking the car. He'd said he wouldn't, as long as I gave him a fiver. I told him to stuff off, so he'd put the price up to seven quid. I didn't really trust him but I didn't really have much of a choice.

When I pulled up in front of Paul's driveway I stayed sitting in the Fiesta, not wanting to get out straight away. I nursed my throbbing hand which had started bleeding again. A small, red stain flowered against the white gauze. I'd told myself that at least the blood still looked healthy, nice and opaque, but it didn't take away the ache. The voice (Paul's voice?) inside my head was quiet. I was now supposed to walk up Paul's driveway, knock on his front door and wait for him to answer. That was the plan. But I wasn't sure exactly what my reaction would be if he answered the door wearing his new Nine Inch Nails T-shirt. Even less if he wasn't.

I didn't believe in ghosts; my father had always claimed to have seen one but I just saw it as another one of his stories. I didn't believe him, so I guess I didn't believe in this kind of thing either. I didn't believe in magic, Uri Geller, fairies at the bottom of the garden or that you could communicate with somebody by using thoughts alone. And that was the reason why I was sitting in the car, not yet willing to knock on Paul's front door.

As I'd driven through town I'd heard this voice babbling away excitedly inside my head, this voice that claimed to be Paul. Okay, I'd told it. If you're Paul then you've got to prove it to me. I'm on my way to your house now, and when I get there and knock on your door I want you to be wearing your new Nine Inch Nails T-shirt. So if I now got out of the car, walked up the driveway, knocked on the front door and Paul answered it wearing his new Nine Inch Nails T-shirt, then I guess that meant I should also start believing in fairies and stuff, right? Whereas if I knocked on the front door and he wasn't wearing his new Nine Inch Nails T-shirt it would only go to prove I was cracking up, and I don't think I really wanted that to happen either.

That's why I was quite happy sitting where I was for the moment thank you very much.

I was considering the idea of maybe just driving away and never finding out, when Paul's face suddenly appeared underneath the net curtains at his living room window. My heart instantly picked up speed. I could only see his face, I couldn't see what he was wearing. He thumped on the glass and waved before disappearing.

I had my hand on the ignition key, so close to running away. Then, within a matter of seconds, he reappeared at the front door and came charging down the drive. I turned away, not wanting to see what he was wearing, not wanting to admit I'd already noticed his top was green, not wanting to admit that I knew full well his new Nine Inch Nails T-shirt was black.

He tapped on the driver's side window. I didn't look at him. I didn't want my full view to confirm what I could see out of the corner of my eye. The green jumper could only mean one thing: I was going insane.

'What're you doing sitting in there, Chris? Aren't you coming in for a drink or something?'

He was grinning at me. I could see out of the corner of my eye that absurd grin of his. Grinning at me above that awful green jumper of his.

He tapped again. He tried the door handle, but it was locked, and I wouldn't open it. 'Come on, Chris. What's wrong with you, mate? Are you still ill or something?'

I looked at him then, and took the non-T-shirtness of his green jumper full in my face. I slowly wound down the window. 'I think I'm going crazy, Paul.'

He shook his head. 'Nar, no way. I bet you you're not.' And with that he grabbed the bottom of his jumper and pulled it up over his head. He was wearing his new Nine Inch Nails T-shirt underneath. He lowered his jumper slightly so I could see the grin splashed across his face, bigger than ever.

– Surprise – he said, inside my head.

A huge feeling of relief washed over me, leaving goosebumps. I felt like a leper miraculously cured. Of course, I'd known all along I wasn't mad. It wasn't as if I'd truly believed I was cracking up, the very idea was ridiculous. I'd realised right from the start that there was a simple explanation . . .

And the feeling which had washed over me now left me cold.

Paul reached in through the Fiesta's open window, unlocked the door and tried to prise me out of the car. But I wouldn't budge an inch.

'What's wrong with you now?' he asked.

'Nothing.' I pulled the car door closed. 'I just want to go home, that's all.'

Paul was shocked. He opened the door again. 'You can't go home yet. Not now.'

– Don't you think this is dead cool? – said the voice in my head.

'Don't do that,' I said nastily.

– Why not? –

'I said, don't do it. It freaks me out, okay?'

Paul pulled a face. He sat himself down on the pavement, wrapping his arms around his knees, looking in at me through the open door. 'I can't believe you,' he said. He shook his head as if to prove it. 'Don't

61

you think this is cool? Don't you think this is probably the most incredible thing that's ever happened to you in your life?'

I shrugged. I didn't know. I didn't know how to react. I didn't know what to think. I was relieved I wasn't going insane. But . . . I, you know, I . . . I couldn't even find the thoughts to think.

'I thought you always wanted to be special,' Paul said. 'I thought you always said to me that you wanted to have adventures like those people in the books you read and do all the kinds of things they do. Because at the moment, Chris, I've got to admit to feeling pretty special.'

– Pretty bloody special – he added.

I shook my head, partly in denial, partly to get his voice out of it. 'It's not that . . .' I started.

'It's not what?' He held his hands up in a despairing gesture. He couldn't understand why I wasn't feeling the same kind of thrill he was. 'Come on, Chris,' he said. 'What's wrong? I don't get it.'

I shrugged again. 'I don't know. I can't explain it.'

He glared at me. 'So try. Go on, I dare you.'

I took a deep breath, desperate to make Paul understand. 'I don't believe in ghosts,' I said.

Paul was confused. 'And?'

'I don't believe in ghosts,' I repeated. I gripped the steering wheel, shaking my head. 'I don't believe in fairies,' I told him. I saw him about to open his mouth and rode straight over the top of his words. 'Or magic. I don't believe in the bogey man, or . . . or dragons and unicorns. Or anything like that.'

'But . . .'

'So if I don't believe in them, then I can't believe in this either.' I turned to look him in the eye. 'I don't believe in ghosts, so I don't believe in telepathy.'

Paul simply smiled. Then he started laughing.

– Tough – he told me. – I do –

Chapter Six

Over the years my mother has developed this uncanny knack for being able to annoy me.

'As long as you don't come home in the same state you did last Friday.'

She would never leave anything alone, she didn't know how to let sleeping dogs lie, she would forever be picking at the scab.

'You're lucky your father and I are even letting you out after *that* performance.'

I sat quietly at the kitchen table and let her get on with it. It was easy enough to do, I'd done it plenty of times before.

'I hope you're not planning on going to another party.'

'No, I've told you, we're just going to get a couple of videos out at Paul's house.' Which, I admit, wasn't the whole truth. But there was no way I was about to tell her exactly what the whole truth was. Not that she would have believed me even if I had.

'Well, just remember what I've told you.'

'Yes, Mum,' I sighed. It wasn't as if I could forget. I'd heard it so many times over the last few days I felt as if I'd had it branded on to my memory. She hadn't let up all week.

'Just so long as you do.'

My mother was shorter than me by at least three inches, but she still knew she was boss. She knew how to scare me as well – it was whenever she got angry and it was in her eyes. They became fiery and as she was telling you off she'd fix you in her gaze, daring you to look away, daring you to make her angrier, her eyes rapidly flicking back and forth between yours. But at the moment she wasn't telling me off, she was just being annoying.

'Oh, and by the way,' she added. 'I found an odd sock of yours in the wash today. Try and find the other one, please. It's probably stuffed at the bottom of your wardrobe, knowing you.'

I kept my head down.

She dished the meal up onto the plates (definitely no chicken done in breadcrumbs tonight) and called through to my father that it was getting cold.

My father walked into the kitchen and closed the door behind him. 'Robert doesn't want anything to eat,' he said. 'He'll wait and see how he feels later on.'

My father was a slim man, a little bit taller than me. Apart from his ever-expanding bald spot I don't think my father was really showing any signs of aging. Not that I think he'd ever grown up properly anyway, he was still a big kid at heart. Still wanting play-fights with me even though I was eighteen, still telling naff jokes and inventing incredible stories. In fact I reckon his hair was the only thing he *had* grown out of.

'Do you have to wear those sunglasses at the table, Christopher?' my mother asked.

I took them off reluctantly, replacing them with my normal pair.

'Thank you,' my mother said, and began to eat.

'They're growing back quicker than I expected them to,' my father said.

I touched my eyebrows self-consciously. There were bits of stubble coming through, but I couldn't make up my mind whether or not the stubble looked any less stupid than having no eyebrows at all.

'I still think a couple of small plasters painted black would be just as good as your sunglasses,' my father told me with a grin.

I offered him his sarcastic grin back and he laughed at me.

'You could put an advert in the Lost and Found section of the paper,' the comedian continued. 'Lost: One pair of eyebrows. Answers to the name of "Bushy".'

I nearly smiled, but managed to stop myself just in time. I wasn't in the mood for smiling. I had too many things on my mind. I had things on my mind that I wasn't too sure I really wanted there.

'Are you going out tonight, then?' my father asked building himself a chip butty.

'Just round to Paul's,' I replied.

My father looked surprised. 'Round to Paul's, eh?'

I nodded. 'We're getting a couple of videos out.'

'I didn't think you and Paul were getting on too well at the minute,' he said carefully.

I shrugged. 'I just haven't seen him for a couple of days, that's all.' I caught him giving my mother one of his irritating 'knowing glances' and added: 'We've both been a bit busy. You know, what with looking for jobs and that.'

He didn't buy it, I could tell by his face. He knew something was wrong between us. He knew it wasn't like me not to return Paul's calls, and completely unheard of for us to go three days without seeing each other. But I'd had a lot to think about since Tuesday. I still didn't know if I'd come to terms with what had happened yet, and that was why I needed to see Paul tonight. I'd reached some sort of conclusion and really needed to know if he agreed. Not that I could explain any of this to my father. I wouldn't have known how to.

My mother was good enough to change the subject. 'How's your hand feeling?' she asked. 'Any better?'

I nodded. 'Yeah. It's stopped bleeding at long last.' Which was true. And the pain had vanished as completely as the headache had done.

'I still can't understand why you didn't let the doctor look at it when he was here.'

'Because he didn't really cut it picking up broken glass,' my father interupted, aiming his knowing glance at me this time. 'It's too clean a cut. And Dr Wheeler would have told him so.'

Once again I was amazed by the fact that you simply couldn't get anything past my father. And it made me wonder just who the hell was the *real* mind reader in the family. But I stayed quiet, ate quickly and cursed Dr Wheeler. All that doctor seemed to have done for me was cause trouble.

The three of us sat around the table eating quietly. My father told my mother about his day at work, my mother told him about her day at home. I joined in briefly with my efforts at job hunting. I tried to make it sound as sarcastic as possible, still wanting them to know how much I hated the idea of looking for work. I was in the middle of some lie about McDonald's not needing any staff when it happened.

– Chris! –

I shut up mid-sentence. My parents both looked up at me from their meals, expecting me to continue. But it came again. Louder this time.

– Chris! Help! –

'Chris . . .?' my mother began.

And when Paul shouted in panic a third time I jumped up from the table, my knife falling to clatter on the tiled floor.

'I've got to go.' And I knew I had to, but I stood there not quite being able to get my legs to do anything, not quite knowing exactly *what* to do.

'Chris . . .!'

'Dad. Can I borrow the car?'

'What's the sudden hurry? Surely you can at least finish your tea? Your mother's spent time cooking it so . . .'

'But Dad, I . . .'

'Oh, let him go if he wants to,' my mother said. 'But I'm not saving it for him. It's going straight in the bin.'

'Please, Dad. It's really important.' I knew I was getting them mad. Meal times were kind of sacred in our house; dinner at twelve, tea at five, the only time the whole family got together. 'Please?' I was already pulling on my shoes.

My father sighed. 'The keys are on top of the fridge,' he told me. 'But this is the last time you do this, Chris. In the future when your mother cooks you a meal, you eat it, okay?'

I grabbed the keys. 'Thanks, Dad.' I was halfway through the back door. 'Sorry, Mum.'

I sprinted up the drive and jumped into the Fiesta. Paul was in trouble. Big trouble. And I needed to get to him fast. But there was no way I could explain how I knew this to my parents.

– Chris! –

  – I'm coming, I'm coming –

  – Quick, Chris. Hurry –

The traffic lights at the top of Town Road forced me to stop. Damn. *Damn*. My heart was hammering in my chest. Come on come on come on.

  – *Chris*! –

  – I know, I know, I'm trying –

The instant they turned green I was away, pushing the little Fiesta for all it was worth, slamming up through the gears.

I brought the car to a bit of a screeching halt, bumping up on to the grass verge of Carvard Avenue at the back entrance to Cleeston Comprehensive. The high gate was locked, the playing field beyond empty.

– Where are you, Paul? I can't see you –

– Believe me, I'm coming. I'm coming just about as fast as I can –

His voice sounded slightly different inside my head. It sounded cleaner; very crisp, very clear. It was as if when he spoke normally the sound had to fight against the air in between his mouth and my ear, it had to fight against the movement of his lips and the wax in my ears to be heard. But when he spoke straight into my head there was nothing to taint the clarity of his voice. Except maybe disbelief.

I got out of the car and went to the mesh fence that ran along the edge of the field separating the school from the world outside. There was still no sign of Paul, but this was where he'd told me to wait. I scanned the scene searching for him. I had a perfect view from here, the field dipping down slightly before me, a narrow path leading from the gate by my side all the way along the edge of the field to the back of the drama hall. I'd walked that pathway too many times to remember, to and from school, down the side of the football and hockey pitches, past the tennis courts and into the main square of buildings. It was funny to think I'd never drag myself down that path first thing in the morning anymore. Funny, and kind of sad I guessed. I wondered if Newcastle University would look anything like the comp.

And then Paul appeared, running. He darted around the side of the drama hall and sprinted straight into the tennis courts, trying to cut the long corner the path would have forced him to take. He was going full tilt. – Oh God, oh God, oh God – resounded in my head. Bob Moody and his beefy mate St. Pierre were close behind him. They were a long way away and I couldn't see their faces, but the two lumbering hulks couldn't be anyone else.

I could do nothing but watch, I was too far away to help.

– Run. Run! –

– What the hell d' you think I'm doing? – Then: – Shit! –

Paul looked as though he'd faltered in his stride. I strained my eyes to see what was happening. He made a sudden leap at the mesh fence of the tennis courts. What on earth did he think he was doing? This was no time to get clever. But then I noticed the other entrance to the tennis courts was locked and realised Paul had got himself trapped in there by trying to cut that corner. I cringed as I saw the other two lads close in on him.

St. Pierre grabbed one of Paul's ankles and started trying to pull him off the fence. Paul must have been clinging on with all his strength because the fence bucked and swayed beneath him but he didn't let go. Frustration rose in me because I couldn't see clearly what was happening. I was clinging on to my own mesh fence almost as hard as Paul must have been clinging on to his, my fingers hooked through the holes like claws.

I don't know how but Paul somehow managed to break free from St. Pierre's grip and was again scrambling up the fence. Bob Moody suddenly made a run back through the tennis courts, going back the way they'd come, hoping to trap Paul on the other side. St. Pierre had hold of the fence and shook it so hard I thought he was going to rip it out of the ground. Paul bounced and boogied like a rag doll, still clinging, still making his way to the top. Bob Moody was coming round the side. And as Paul pulled himself over the top St. Pierre rattled the fence hard enough to throw him off. I watched in horror as Paul fell. He shrieked inside my head as he hit the grass below.

– You okay? – He wasn't moving. I ran to the high gate and started climbing, trying to get to him even though there was still the length of a football pitch between us. – Paul? Paul? – I was a hell of a lot further away than Bob Moody.

– Yeah, yeah. I think so – He was getting to his feet. I stopped climbing, hanging halfway up the wrought-iron of the gate, completely gripped by the scene unfolding before me. I could see Paul was holding his side. – That hurt – he told me.

Bob Moody surprised him; Paul didn't realise how close the kid was.

– Watch out – I thought, too late.

But somehow Paul managed to dodge him. And was running again, if a little unsteadily this time. He ran around the goal net, on to the pitch. I was sure Bob Moody was too close behind for him to be able to make it all the way across the field. I began climbing the gate again. St. Pierre was now also on the field.

– I'm coming –

– Start the car –

– You'll never make it –

– Start the car, Chris! –

I dropped back down from the gate, but didn't make any kind of a move towards the Fiesta. I couldn't. My hands were fists, clenching and unclenching, urging Paul on. Bob Moody looked like he was within touching distance of him. Paul made it to the halfway line, Bob Moody just a step behind him, St. Pierre still only in the box but gaining fast. If Paul fell he was a dead man.

– I know, I know – he told me.

I could see his face now. He looked panic-stricken, but so very determined. His teeth were gritted. His hair streamed out behind him, flapping almost in Bob Moody's face. But he looked worse than Paul did, his cheeks puffing in and out as he fought for his breath. I felt a glimmer of hope. The big kid was tiring. It was like a contest of wills, and I suddenly got the idea Paul would win because the will for him to escape was far stronger than Bob Moody's will to catch him.

'Come on, run,' I hissed. – Run –

– The car, Chris. Start the car –

I couldn't move. Nothing could drag me away. I watched as Paul steadily got closer and closer. Was Bob Moody falling back slightly? They started to climb the little rise in the field. They passed the nearest goalmouth, Paul's arms and legs pumping just about as fast as they could go. His jacket was hanging off his elbows, filling up behind him like a miniature parachute as he ran. But he was making it.

– Run, run, run – I was jumping up and down. – Yes! Come on, come on – I was shaking the mesh fence.

Paul fell.

I didn't see how it happened, he just tripped, his legs falling away beneath him. I shouted. I immediately jumped at the fence and started to climb. He sprawled forward, crumpling up into a ball.

And Bob Moody was upon him . . . But was running so fast himself he couldn't stop in time. I saw the look of surprise on his face as he charged into the heap of Paul's body, his weight thrown forward. He hit the ground face first. His back bent and his legs flipped over his head in the most bizarre kind of somersault I've ever seen.

'Get up,' I shouted. – Get up –

They both did. Paul was on his feet first. Bob Moody was slow moving, he looked hurt. They were only yards from the gate.

'Start the' – car for Christ's sake –

But his fall had given St. Pierre chance to make up some ground and as Paul leapt up at the gate, the other kid once again grabbed at his ankle.

'Start it, Chris. Start it now!'

'Keep hold of him. Don't let him go.'

'Let him go, St. Pierre. Leave him alone.'

'The car, Chris!'

'I've got him. I've got him.'

'Get off my leg.'

'Don't let him go.'

St. Pierre was not going to let Paul slip away this time. He pulled on his leg with all his weight. He hung from it. And Paul was clinging on to the gate just as hard. His fingers were bright red as they gripped the bars, his knuckles white. I knew there was no way he'd be able to hang on when Bob Moody got hold of his other leg.

I looked around frantically for a stick. I couldn't see one. There had to be one somewhere.

'Get off! Get off me.'

74

'You're dead, Stewart.'

'Don't let him go.'

I ran to the car. I fumbled only briefly beneath the driver's seat before snatching the bright yellow 'Stop-lock' steering lock from under there. It was better than any stick.

'. . . dickhead . . .'

'. . . dead man . . .'

'. . . tosser . . .'

I ran back to the gate. St. Pierre was too busy to see me. I thrust the long, metal rod through the bars in the gate just about as hard as I could. It rammed him in the gut. Then I swung it up to smack into his forearm. He screamed and let go of Paul. Paul didn't need a second invitation to get his backside over that gate.

We piled into the car, the air thick with shouts and curses. St. Pierre was holding his arm, screaming at us. Bob Moody still wasn't even at the gate yet, but he was hollering just the same. Paul was gasping for breath, sweating hard, but he still managed to conjure up the strength to be able to lean out of the window long enough to flick the 'Vs' as I drove away.

We drove to Paul's house. I was shaking slightly, the after-effects of my shooting adrenalin causing a trembling in my guts. Paul got his breath back and then started laughing. By the time we reached his house he was as full of bravado as ever.

'Did you see St. Pierre run? I was like,' he blew his breath out making a big, exasperated sound. 'He ran like the wind. He was just,' he made a fast, rushing sound, karate-chopping the air with his hand. 'And I was,' he panted loudly, giving it all the arm movements. 'But I knew I'd lose them if I dodged into the comp.'

I didn't answer, I just wanted my quivering stomach to sit still for a while.

I parked the Fiesta in Paul's driveway and we headed upstairs to his bedroom. He grabbed a couple of Cokes from the kitchen on the way. I took the cat's place on the bed and Paul slumped down with his back against the wardrobe doors. He was still shaking his head and laughing quietly to himself.

'They chased me all the way from the off-licence on Johnson Street. I went in to get a couple of cans for tonight and wham! they were on me. I must've run for miles. I had to run round the comp twice waiting for you to turn up.'

'I told you. I warned you Bob Moody was seeing Jane Lois-Lane, and you wouldn't listen.'

'She was the one who started it. She was the one with her hand on my backside.'

'Tell that to Bob Moody.'

'I did try,' he laughed. He took a gulp of his Coke and held the cold can against his red and sweaty cheek. 'I wonder who spragged me up.'

'Probably that Laura.'

He nodded. 'Yeah. Probably.'

'Cow.'

There was a silence between us then. We sat drinking our Cokes.

I watched Paul as he stared at the can in his hand. The silence stretched. I could tell Paul was uncomfortable, that there were things that needed to be said but he didn't quite know how to broach the subject. I was no better; something about us had definitely changed.

I'd phoned him that afternoon and told him that we needed to talk. I'd needed time to think things over. On my own.

'I bought the new Radiohead CD yesterday,' Paul said. 'D'you wanna listen to it?'

'Yeah, shove it on. Is it as good as their other stuff?'

'Not as good as The Bends, but still pretty smart.' He had his back to me, putting the disc in the machine when he said, 'I wasn't sure whether you'd come tonight. You know, to help me with those two.'

'I wasn't sure whether you were lying or not. I thought you might've just been trying to get me to believe in it. To get me to admit it was real.'

He still had his back to me. 'Do you believe in it?' he asked.

I thought about it only briefly before saying, 'I don't think there's any way I can't, is there? I mean, I've been using it myself all night, haven't I?'

Paul nodded. He turned around to face me now, sitting back down again. The music burst out of his speakers.

'It just freaked me out at first,' I continued. 'I thought I was cracking up or something, you know? And I still don't get it. I still don't understand why it's happened.'

'Because we became blood brothers.'

'Well, yeah, obviously. And that's what the headache and every-thing was about, wasn't it? But I mean, it can't happen to everybody who becomes blood brothers, can it? Loads of people become blood brothers and none of them go running around talking in each other's heads, do they?'

Paul shrugged. 'Maybe . . .'

'Oh, come on. They can't, can they? Not really. Somebody would've said something by now, don't you think?'

'Yeah. I guess so.'

'So I reckon there's a reason behind it. We've got this power for a purpose.'

Paul frowned. 'How d'you mean?'

I took a deep breath. This was what I'd decided, this was the speech I'd prepared over the past couple of days. I tried to get my words into some sort of order.

'Okay,' I said. 'I'm not claiming that there's this big, omnipotent, good guy who's looked down on us and has seen this massive catas-trophe fast approaching and said, "Well hey, we can't have that happening now, can we? Let's give these two kids a wonderous power and they'll stop it from happening." But,' I said, watching Paul's face, 'but on the other hand I really can't believe someone's said, "Here you go, lads. Have a fairly amusing but fairly useless power to play with," either.'

I couldn't read any kind of reaction from Paul. He was looking at his can of Coke.

I continued anyway. 'I mean, I don't even know if we were given it by some Mr Good guy, or even if anybody gave it to us at all. For all I know we might have got it accidentally. But if it was an accident, then I really believe it has to have been accidentally on purpose.' I realised I'd been waving my hands about as I'd been speaking, and so sat on them, forcing myself to shut up even though I knew I wanted to say so much more. I finished with: 'If you know what I mean.'

Paul wouldn't take his eyes off the can in his hand. The track on the CD finished and the brief silence between songs spun itself out for what seemed like an age.

The music kicked in again, guitars first. I watched Paul. He shrugged, then nodded, then frowned, went to open his mouth, but closed it again. He rotated the can slowly in his hand, still staring at it. Radiohead played on.

'That's what I wanted to come round and say,' I told him, feeling slightly embarrassed. The music crashed and thudded in the background. The cat jumped up into my lap, wanting its comfy spot on the bed back. I shoved it away.

'You're always so serious,' Paul told me. I went to contradict him, but he held up his hand to hush me. 'Just think of what we could do with this power. This is the greatest thing that's ever happened to me. I can't believe we just thought being blood brothers was cool, and then this happened. The whole reason we wanted to be blood brothers in the first place was to make our friendship special, right? And now look at it. How much more special can you get? I reckon we should forget all about your catastrophe stuff and have the time of our lives. Just think about next time I'm getting off with Jane Lois-Lane.' He started laughing. 'Just think of the running commentary I'm gonna be giving you.'

I smiled despite myself.

'Come on, Chris,' he grinned. 'Let's just roll with it. Have a laugh. See what happens.'

I shrugged. I knew what he meant, but I had this certain niggling at the back of my head . . .

'Just think about the kind of stuff we can do,' Paul said. 'I mean, for starters you're going to help me pass my driving test.'

'Yeah? And how did you figure that one out?'

'Well there's no way I'm gonna waste my time learning the highway code, is there? Not when you can just send the answers straight into my head.'

'If only we'd become blood brothers before the exams.'

'Oh, man.' Paul rolled his eyes. 'That would've been excellent.'

I was laughing as well now. 'At least you might have passed then.'

Paul nodded. 'Yeah,' he grinned at me. 'But d'you see what I mean? Tonight was just an example of what we can do with this power. You can come and save me from jealous boyfriends any time you want to from now on.'

I shook my head. 'No, no way. I'm not getting mixed up in your love-life. It's always been way too scary for me. Tonight I was just paying you back. I don't owe you one any more.'

'What d'you mean you don't owe me one any more? I got myself shot for you. You can't say that driving a car for me is equal to getting shot for you.'

'Okay, I tell you what,' I said. 'When this massive catastrophe comes along I'll let it happen to you. And then when I save you from it we'll be equal, okay?'

'As long as you do save me.'

'Of course I will. Trust me.' I leaned over and punched his arm lightly. 'And when I do,' I said, remembering something from the past, 'You can be sure I'll be shouting *Super Stonner to the rescue!*' I jumped up on his bed and struck my best superhero pose.

Paul fell about laughing. 'You should have shouted it at St. Pierre when you smacked him one with the steering lock.'

I nodded vigorously. 'Just call me your friendly, neighbourhood speccy git.'

We messed around a bit, jumping about, play fighting and shouting until we were sweating and panting as hard as we'd been after our encounter with Bob Moody and St. Pierre. Then we slumped back down on to the floor and just sat grinning at each other. I still thought things had changed between us, but now I understood how. I was hit by a sudden premonition that the two of us would always be friends, that in ten years time we'd be sitting together, messing about, laughing, sharing the good times. I realised that even when I did go to Newcastle there was no way I was going to get rid of this guy. And that made me feel good. Admittedly I didn't know where the two of us would *be* sitting and laughing, but as long as Paul was watching my back, I didn't really care.

'So, does this mean you now believe in ghosts and stuff?' Paul asked. 'Magic, and fairies at the bottom of the garden?'

I shrugged. – Maybe –

'Daaad?'

'Hmm?'

'Can you remember that ghost you once told me about? The one you said you saw at work?'

'The one at Abbey House?'

'Yeah, that's it. What exactly happened again?'

PART THREE

Chapter Seven

It was the last day of July, and the month was leaving us on a glorious Tuesday afternoon. The day was very bright; the sun sparkled and winked off windows, door handles and the spokes of bicycle wheels. Sunglasses were out in force. There was the tiniest of breezes to help make the heat bearable. It was easily the best day of the summer so far, and seemed like just about the perfect day to be cheating on your driving test to me.

– The stopping distance at forty miles per hour? –

– Thirty-six metres –

– Cheers –

The nearest pub to the test centre was The Breech. I was sitting at a wooden picnic table in the beer garden with a copy of *The Highway Code* open in front of me. My attention alternated between the book and my pint.

Paul hadn't exactly given me a running commentary on the driving part of his test, but the occasional swear word or two had drifted into my head, and more than a few abusive remarks about other road-users. He'd told me there'd been no real problems though, the examiner hadn't made any marks on his clipboard so far. Now all he had to do was make it through the question-and-answer session unscathed. Which wouldn't be at all difficult with me flipping through the pages of *The Highway Code*.

When I'm overtaking a parked car, how much room do I give it?

– Er, not sure. Please hold the line – I hummed him a little tune as I flipped. – Okay, found it. Give enough room for the driver to open his door –

– You sure? –

– That's what it says here –

I took a sip of my pint, smirking to myself. I could just imagine the officious look on the examiner's face as he asked the questions. Important questions which gave him power over wannabe drivers everywhere, questions which decided their fate. I imagined him in his shipshape shirt and tidy tie, holding his clipboard close to his chest, the sign of his authority over Paul. The authority which we at the moment were making a complete mockery of. And it gave me quite an uplifting feeling to tell the truth.

– He's gonna test me on road signs next – Paul told me. – He's got this flip book full of them –

– Don't worry – I replied, turning to the back pages of the booklet. We've got just as many as he has –

– Okay, here they come. What's that one with the two cars on it? One red, one black –

I scanned the pages in front of me. – No overtaking –

– Thought so. And the one that looks like breasts? –

– Uneven road surface –

– That's the one –

The examiner showed Paul at least eight or nine signs. I told Paul each and every one of them. Of course I knew it was wrong to cheat, and so I felt appropriately remorseful. The driving test had been set up to help keep drivers in check, to make sure that whoever was allowed on the road was a capable and controlled driver. It was set up for the safety of all. The way Paul and I were flouting the system was irresponsible, the way we were treating the examiner disrespectful. So I did feel suitably guilty. I felt conscience-stricken and suddenly had the urge to call the whole thing off, telling Paul that I didn't want any part of his heinous and sinful crime.

Okay, so I'm lying. So I really just took another gulp of my pint and smirked.

I hadn't stayed too long at Paul's house last Friday night; he'd wanted me to go home so that we could talk to each other over the distance between our houses. And we'd talked all through the night. Not only because he'd threatened to invade my dreams with subliminal messages if I fell asleep, but also because neither of us really wanted to stop. What we were doing was quite literally mind-blowing, and we had wanted to revel in the incredible, giddy sensation we'd both been feeling.

85

We'd been like little kids with a new toy. I'd sat all the way through lunch with my parents that Saturday whilst giving Paul a running commentary on my father's magnificent chip butty building skills. Not because it was interesting but simply because it was something to say, another reason to use the power. Paul had gone with his mother to the supermarket that same afternoon and had given me the lowdown on the price of everything he was putting in the trolley, of how attractive the checkout girls were and of how upset he was when his mother wouldn't let him stand in the queue served by the best-looking one.

– That's the whole point of going to supermarkets – he'd moaned.

– That's the only reason I go to Tesco's – I'd agreed.

I admit that it had been a fairly rapid turnaround of feelings on my part. One minute our telepathy had scared me because of its implications, the next I'd seen it as some kind of miracle, and then it had simply become a toy. And I guess I could tell you that I wasn't really a hypocrite, I could say that I was still thinking about my been-given-it-for-a-reason theory, that all this playing was actually my way of honing the power to a fine art. I could say that what I was doing was practising the power, readying myself for the day when we'd need to use it to battle against the forces of evil or whatever. But that, I'm afraid, would be another lie. Quite simply, Paul and I were having a blast.

We hadn't really let up for the past couple of days. If an opportunity had arisen for us to use the power, we'd used it. And even if one hadn't, we'd still used it. Like yesterday when Paul had gone to the Job Centre. He'd let me know that there were no decent jobs going and I'd had an extra couple of hours in bed. Since Friday night I don't think we'd actually spoken more than two or three words to each other in the usual, *physical* way.

And then Paul gave a little whoop inside my head. – Yeah, yeah, yeah! I'm great, I'm cool, I've passed –

I sent him a whoop back.

– Get the drinks ready – he told me. – I'm on my way –

– All righty then – I stood up to go to the bar, grinning hugely. I couldn't believe I'd been worried about how this summer was going to turn out. Surely it was shaping up to be the best one ever.

Chapter Eight

I admit it was cheap, and I admit it was nasty, but it was one of those opportunities that I simply wasn't able to pass up. I just had to do it. If I hadn't it would have been like closing my eyes as Lady Godiva rode by. And I reckon she deserved it. Paul agreed. An eye for an eye, he said. Or rather an eyebrow for an eyebrow, ha, ha, ha.

It was the day after our driving test victory. Paul was complaining because his parents wouldn't let him use the car as and when he wanted it, or rather because he'd had to walk into town. We were in the McDonald's on Market Street, the Job Centre was only down the road but it didn't look as if we were going to be able to make it that far today. We'd been hijacked by a quarter pounder deluxe (with fries).

Getting a job really didn't seem important any more. At the back of my mind was a twinge of guilt, a little, nervous tick that kept on reminding me that I'd have no money when I got to university. But it was always too small and too brief a thought to leave any lasting impression. It should really have been Paul who was the one worrying about getting a job anyway. He was the one who wasn't going away, he was the one who was officially unemployed. But I guess neither of us really believed we actually needed a job. We were surrounded by this glow of optimism. We were on top of the world. We felt incredible, untouchable, immortal. And it was all thanks to the power.

The younger kids had also broken up from school by this time and the restaurant was packed out with them and their Happy Meals, so Paul and I had to stand and hunker over our burgers next to the window that overlooked the street, using the sill as a table. Scooping the ketchupy, mayonnaisey, iceberg-lettucey mess up from the bottom of the polystyrene box and licking it off your fingers is a must. Getting gunk at the corners of your mouth is all part of the experience. You can't relax and properly enjoy yourself if you've got people looking in at the window, watching you, staring at the relish on your chin. That was why I had my back to the window, leaning against the sill. And that was why it was Paul who spotted Jane Lois-Lane and her friend, Laura.

– Oh, no –

– What? –

– Jane Lois-Lane and Laura – Paul sent.

I ducked my head into my shoulders as if it would help to hide me. – Have they seen us? –

– 'fraid so –

– Oh, no –

Laura was quite literally the last person I wanted to see. I could feel myself beginning to blush already. I pushed my glasses as high up my nose as they would go, using the back of my hand so I wouldn't smear the lenses with fingerprints of mayonnaise, hoping the frames would cover my eyebrows. Not that they were looking particularly stupid any more, they'd grown back pretty well. It was just that I knew her eyes would keep flicking up to them. I knew she'd want to see how her handiwork had turned out.

I felt as though this girl was one up on me. And in a sense I guess it really was one-nil to her. But that was what hurt the most; the fact that she had managed to find a chink in my armour. I saw her as the only person who had managed to scratch the invincibility I was feeling.

– Don't tell them I'm here, Paul, will you? –

He looked at me quizzically, nibbling on a single fry. – Why, where're you going? –

– To the toilet. Let me know when they've gone, okay? –

– Don't worry about Laura –

– I'm not worried –

– She's not worth it. She's a right snoopy reject –

– I know, I know. I just need the loo, that's all –

He shook his head at me, shoving more fries into his mouth. – You can't lie to me – he sent. – I can read your mind, remember? –

I ignored the comment and instead told him not to speak when his mouth was full, then legged it upstairs to the toilet. Paul chided me all the way.

What he didn't realise, and what you probably don't realise either, is that I wasn't actually running away. Not really. It was all part of my plan. You might think that I was hiding myself in the gents because I was scared Laura would make me feel so very crushed and humiliated. Well, admittedly, I knew she'd make some smarmy comment designed to embarrass me, but hey, I'd hate you to think that I wouldn't be able to handle it. Of course I'd be able to handle it. Of course I'd instantly be able to think of some witty put-down so good and so sharp it'd slam her fat mouth shut and knock her on to her even fatter backside, both at the same time.

Honest.

And if you don't believe me I don't really care. Because this is my story, I'm the narrator, and I can tell it any way I want to. Okay?

So there I was, *waiting* in the gents, for just the right moment to spring my plan into action. This particular McDonald's only had the two toilets upstairs, there was no restaurant area, that was all down-stairs. The stairs led you up to a narrow corridor that overlooked Market Street and had three doors off it; the ladies, the gents and a cleaner's cupboard. I'd seen the mop bucket standing outside the cleaner's cupboard as I'd come up the stairs (but I'd hoped all along one would be there).

I hung around near the hand basins for a while, but after getting some funny looks from a couple of blokes I decided to lock myself into a cubicle. Paul was sending to me all the time: – Jane Lois-Lane thinks I'm looking nice today –

– And are you? –

– Of course –

91

– What's Laura saying? – I asked.

– Not much, she just wanted to know where you were –

– And what did you tell her? –

– I just said you were on the jobby –

– You what? –

– I mean, at the Job Centre –

I've got to admit that I felt a bit stupid sitting in those Mctoilets like that. It was lucky I wasn't hiding or I would have felt even more stupid. If I'd been hiding it would have proved that Laura was getting to me, and getting to me badly. It would mean that I wasn't any better than I had been when this toad of a girl had shaved my eyebrows off at Matty Harker's party. And almost two weeks had passed since then. Almost two weeks in which the power had made me a pretty special person in my eyes.

If I'd been hiding then I would have probably been disgusted at myself for losing, in one fell swoop, that feeling of immortality and invincibility Paul and I had been nurturing over the past few days.

– Are you coming down or what? – Paul asked.

– Not yet, I've got a plan – I told him.

– You what? –

– Just let me know when Laura leaves –

– Why? –

– Just tell me, at the exact moment she steps foot outside the door, tell me –

I had to wait another five minutes or so. I hovered in the narrow corridor. A couple of customers gave me a couple more funny looks, but no members of staff appeared. The tiled floor had recently been mopped, hence the bucket of sludgy water, and a window had been left open to help the floor dry with the warm summer breeze. I kept glancing down on to the street below; I really didn't want to miss my opportunity. Paul'd better not let me down.

– What's happening? – I asked Paul.

– Jane Lois-Lane's just giving me loads of rubbish about Bob Moody. You know, the sort of stuff I could really do without hearing. Yes, Jane, I know he's big. Yes, Jane, I know he wants to smash my face in –

– Are they getting ready to leave yet? –

– Yeah. Jane's just giving me her phone number

– Tell me when –

– Okay –

– Exactly when –

– Okay, okay. Get ready then –

My heart was beating hard enough for me to feel it. A big mischievous grin was spreading its crooked way from ear to ear.

– Here they come – Paul sent. – Here they come –

I was standing by the open window.

– Nearly there. Getting closer –

I didn't dare put my head out. I had to rely on Paul's instruction.

– Her hand's on the door –

I was holding my breath.

– She's opening it now –

The mop bucket, brimming with filthy water, was in my hands.

– Now! – Paul shouted in my head.

And I tipped the bucket up to let the brown liquid slop rain down from above on the head of Laura The Cow.

I didn't wait to look out of the window, I was down those stairs in a flash. Although I did have time to see and appreciate the thick, lumpy dribbles of murky grit which had spattered on the windowsill. The full restaurant was agog and staring out of the windows when I reached it. It was probably one of the most unreal experiences of my life; a completely silent McDonald's restaurant, even more unreal than the power had first seemed. I wouldn't turn to look at what they were all looking at. I could hear Laura shrieking in a kind of hitching, breathless way.

Slowly, hesitant laughter or gasps of disbelief, came from the adults. All-out belly-laughs and unsuppressed guffaws of delight from the kids. I slipped in between them relatively unnoticed. Paul grabbed my arm and we made our escape via the fire exit.

– Oh my God – Paul sent. He was shaking his head.

– What? – I was suddenly frightened I'd maybe gone too far.

He looked at me, still shaking his head. – I can't believe it –

– What? – I asked, more worried than ever. – You can't believe what? –

– Bullseye! – he sent. And we both howled with laughter.

Chapter Nine

We had kind of given up on bus surfing when it had become apparent that we were never going to beat forty minutes. We had another couple of tries after the failed 'hang-five' incident, but never with as much enthusiasm. And anyway, Paul had had some new ideas since then.

As the summer had drawn towards us and the weather had obviously improved, Paul had spent more and more time coming into Stonner. He would catch the 3C or, if he wasn't able to scrounge the fare out of his mother, would cycle the few miles out of town. The village had been a new place for Paul back then. Most people would maybe not have understood the attraction it had held for him, they might have thought that the town was a much more exciting place. But Paul had more or less adventured-out Cleeston.

Stonner had offered a new perspective. He'd wanted to explore the fields that surrounded the village, he'd wanted to climb the trees, he'd wanted to crouch in a sand bunker, steal the golf ball that came his way and hide it from the little old lady with her electric golf trolley. But most of all what Paul had wanted was a den, a secret place where only the two of us could go, where we could get away from everybody else in the whole world. He'd always told me that one day he was going to run away from home and he needed a place where no one would ever find him.

And so we'd built a den. And it was the best den anybody had ever built, and it had become our secret hiding place. But Paul had never quite been able to pluck up the courage to spend the night there, never mind run away from home.

We used to spend hours at a time in that den, just being happy at having a place away from the rest of the world. Of course, it had never bothered us that we weren't supposed to be there. I don't think it had ever crossed my mind that we were trespassing, although it certainly has done since. Since the day it all came to a rather dramatic end, I mean.

The first thing I remember about that hot, summer day is the barbed wire, nasty and threatening . . .

It didn't gleam even though the sun was very bright. It reached right the way from one end of the hedgerow to the other and was secured to the trunks of the trees with 'U' shaped nails. There were four long, vicious lengths of the dull, spiked wire stretched through the bushes' tangled branches and matted leaves. They were too close together to easily slip in between without getting snagged, and the fourth length was much too high to manage a leg over without risking our balls.

We hadn't expected this.

We'd intended to plunge straight into the cover of the bushes, getting out of sight as soon as possible, but now we were stopped dead in our tracks. For a few short seconds neither of us spoke. We simply stared at the wire.

Then Paul said, 'Bet it's the farmer. I bet he did this.' He'd been smiling as we'd run across the field, but his face had suddenly fallen into a scowl at the sight of the wire. 'He better not've done anything to the den. I'll go mad if he has.'

I cast a furtive glance over my shoulder. I was worried the farmer might be watching us.

'We've got to find a way in,' I told Paul. 'Quick, before anyone sees us.'

Just beyond these bushes was a steep-sided ditch that was deep enough even for Paul to stand up straight in without having his beacon-blond hair poking over the top. The ditch separated the two fields and was dry at the bottom, with the trees and bushes reaching right the way over the top like a canopy. But that wasn't the best bit, not by a long shot. Because when you followed the ditch back towards the lane it got narrower and darker as the foliage became thicker still and disappeared into a tunnel that reached underneath the road. All the way under. The den was actually a huge concrete drainage pipe, and we were able to stay hidden in there because it couldn't be seen from the road; nobody knew it even existed, apart from us. Or so we'd thought.

We'd lined the bottom of the pipe with some old blankets because my mum always complained about dirty clothes, no matter how often she did the washing, and we'd even brought a couple of threadbare pillows to sit on. Also, hidden among the thorny bushes at the top of the ditch's bank, was a black plastic bin liner containing the two dirty mags I'd nicked off my brother.

Paul walked a little way along the wire looking for a way over, around or through. 'We can get over here,' he said.

A massive branch from one of the trees hung low over the wire and reaching his hands up above his head Paul was able to grab hold of it. He made sure he had a good grip, then slowly lifted his legs up to stand precariously on the top length of the wire, the branch bending low, but not dangerously so. From here he was able to turn himself around and then drop down backwards among the bushes on the other side.

He grinned at me. 'No sweat.'

I followed quickly. I was grinning too. Had the farmer really expected to stop us from getting to our den? When had barbed wire ever stopped any self-respecting thirteen-year-old from getting anywhere?

We pushed through the lush, green bushes, trampling down the nettles because this wasn't our usual, well-trodden route through to the ditch. The air was rife with gnats and midges, little dancing clouds of them, and our hair was full of blossoms and leaves. We scrambled down into the ditch. On the opposite side the bushes weren't quite so dense or matted and we could see out into the field beyond. We checked briefly to make sure the farmer was still nowhere in sight, then scuttled along the dry ditch bed towards the den.

Paul led the way. He hurried along, cursing the farmer, making up new noises to describe how much he disliked him. Something still didn't seem quite right to me, although I didn't say anything to Paul. Nervously, I followed him along the bottom of the ditch, but as it led us closer to the den it also seemed to lead us closer to a terrible smell that hung in the air.

'What a stink! What is it?' I asked.

'Probably the farmer's wife,' Paul replied nastily.

'Even she can't smell that bad. It must be . . .'

But Paul grabbed me. 'Shush! I think someone's at the den. I can hear them.'

Only a few metres ahead of us the ditch turned slightly to the left as it veered towards the edge of the field and the tunnel that ran underneath the lane. The bushes hung low at this bend, tumbling their massed leaves and branches down into the ditch, obscuring the view of the entrance to the den. We scooted along the narrow ditch, each wanting the better vantage point. It was obvious somebody was there, we could hear them puffing and panting, talking to themselves. And the smell was really strong. We jostled against each other some more, then managed to peer around or through the bushes. And saw . . .

It was the farmer. The farmer was messing with our den!

He was tipping manure out of black plastic bin liners all over the ditch. The old man was wearing rubber galoshes, big ones that came up past his knees, and thick gloves. He spread the muck with his spade, smearing and plastering it all around the entrance to the den. He patted it down evenly. He tipped out another bag full of cow dung as we watched in horror. He grunted with the effort. And then proceeded to daub it up and down the sides of the ditch, all along the bank. The place was literally swamped in the stuff.

Neither Paul nor I could speak. We watched this old man trashing our den in a kind of daze. I couldn't believe it. What did he think he was doing?

And then Paul shouted, 'Get off our den! Leave our den alone!'

The farmer spun around, his spade riding high up to his shoulder like a baseball bat. He shouted, he swore, his anger as threatening as his spade.

'Run!' I shouted. And did.

Paul wasn't far behind. 'Quick! Get going!'

The dry mud was loose and flaky beneath our scrabbling trainers. The narrowness of the ditch made our escape a scrambling, shoving panic.

'Run! Run!'

Banging into each other, pushing ourselves off the high ditch sides, shouting and urging each other on. But at least we weren't the ones wearing galoshes.

'Get back here, you little thugs. Just wait till I get my hands on you.'

The massive, rubber boot-trousers thokked and slapped madly as the farmer chased us. He waved the dirty spade like a sword above his head.

We made it back to where we'd climbed down in to the ditch. But Paul couldn't climb out, the loose mud kept crumbling away beneath his feet.

'Quick! Get out! Jump!'

He kept on pulling out handfuls of grass and weeds that just weren't able to support his weight. I pushed and shoved at his backside, shouting at him to get going, to move, quickly!

The farmer was still yelling. 'I'll kick your backsides into next year.' There was no way he was able to run as fast as us, but there was no way he looked as though he was going to give up trying, either.

I grabbed Paul's foot and gave him a leg-up to get him out of the ditch. He stood on my shoulder and hauled himself out and on to the bank, then held out his hand for me and pulled as I clambered out myself.

'Go. Go!'

We charged through the bushes, swatting aside the meshed branches, leaves exploding around us.

'You go first,' I told Paul and grabbed hold of the wire to keep it as steady as possible for him.

The branch wasn't as low hanging on this side of the wire and Paul had to jump two or three times before he could grab hold of it. He hefted his legs up to stand on the trembling top length of wire; it boogied and shook beneath him. He tried to turn round, but he'd caught the toe of his trainer on a barb. He jerked and kicked his foot, trying to free it, the wire swaying beneath him.

And all the time I could hear the farmer huffing and puffing behind us. I could hear his grunts as he hauled his fat and wrinkly backside out of the ditch.

'Jump,' I shouted at Paul. 'Just jump!'

And he did. He jumped. He kicked away from the wire to land in a crumpled heap on the grass. The branch he'd been holding literally twanged behind him.

The farmer was crashing through the bushes. I leapt up to grab the still vibrating branch and missed. Paul was shouting, urging me on. I jumped at it again, managed to get a hold, but it was still shaking so badly it shook my fingers right off again. And Paul was screaming at me, pointing behind me. I braced myself to make one final attempt.

'Don't you move a muscle, laddy.' The farmer gripped my shoulder painfully. 'I want a word with you.'

Chapter Ten

Meanwhile . . .

I was sitting trying to out-stare the television set. I was losing. Some terrible daytime soap flickered before my straining eyes which felt as if they were out on stalks. The left one was beginning to water.

– Come on, Paul. Are you getting anything or what? – I asked.

– Don't blink, it might disrupt the image –

– I'm not blinking –

– Just keep staring at the telly –

– I can't for much longer –

– Shhhh. I'm concentrating –

– Admit it, it's not working –

– Just a minute, keep going, I think I'm getting something . . . It's ITV, right? –

I groaned. – Look, we can't do it, okay? – I was blinking furiously.

– Can we leave it now, please? My eyes are killing me –

– Just one more try –

I sighed, taking off my glasses and wiping my eyes with the sleeve of my jumper. – That's what you said ten minutes ago. That's what you said when I could still focus properly –

– Look, Chris. This is serious research we're doing here – Paul sent in his most serious tone of voice. – I want to know exactly what we can and cannot do with this power, okay? –

– Well, we can't send pictures, that's for sure –

– Maybe we can't send moving pictures, maybe that's it. Go find a poster or something to stare at –

– You go find a poster or something to stare at –

I was in a bad mood and I didn't really like this idea of Paul's, this 'research'. I was in a bad mood because we'd originally planned on going for a wander around the shops (Paul wanted a new shirt and I was after a couple of CDs) but I'd been forced to stay in to look after my brother again. 'Just in case he needs anything' my mum had said. Not that I'd believed Robert needed anything at all really, my personal opinion being that he was simply dragging out his illness for as long as possible, for as much sympathy and attention as possible. And then he'd only gone and proved me right by sneaking out of the house five minutes after my mum had left, swearing me to silence on pains of a broken rib or two. So here I was, stuck in the house again, looking after an AWOL brother and messing about with something I thought it was probably best not to mess around with. You wouldn't believe how much I was hoping my mum would come home before Robert did. I couldn't wait for him to go back to work at the garage, because under a car he'd be out of my way.

At the time I didn't quite know why I was feeling nervous and so never mentioned it to Paul. In retrospect I think it was maybe because deep down I still hadn't been able to shake the idea completely from my head that Paul and I had to have been given this power for a reason. During our experiments a little tick at the back of my mind kept on telling me it wasn't a toy. But of course that little tick got filed away with the other little ticks already pushed into the shadowy corners of my head: job, exam results, university, mum's birthday. But then again, what I didn't realise at the time was that this particular little tick wasn't a bad sign after all. Things definitely wouldn't have worked out like they did if it hadn't have been for our research that day.

Paul had pulled the Meg Ryan poster down off his bedroom wall and was trying to send me the picture of her, but with the same lack of success. Unfortunately. The next idea he had was to try and send noises to each other. We messed around with CDs, Paul's beaten-up guitar, sounds from the telly and even belches. Again, without success.

– What about smell? – Paul asked.

– I doubt it –

– See if you can smell this –

I tried. – No, nothing –

– Lucky you – Paul told me. – S.b.ds are always the worst –

We came to the conclusion that all we could send each other was our thoughts, which we heard exactly like the sound of the sender's voice. Like some kind of bizarre ventriloquism. But then Paul had another idea:

– What about if you think of absolutely nothing at all? – he asked.

– Eh? –

– I mean, we're always sending each other stuff, right? Words and that. Well, what if you didn't send to me and I tried to listen in anyway –

– You mean, like *proper* mind-reading? – I asked, already worried by the idea.

– Yeah, that's it –

I shook my head (not that he could see me). – No. I don't think we should try anything like that –

– Why not? –

– It sounds a bit dodgy to me – I sent.

– Don't be soft –

I shrugged (but again he couldn't see me).

He made a rather peculiar sound inside my head.

– What's that meant to be? – I asked.

– A chicken – he told me. – Because that's what you are –

I tried my best to ignore him, but he repeated the noise, louder, just in case I'd missed it first time round.

– Okay, okay. What d'you want me to do? –

And the next thing I knew I was on the living room floor with a pillowcase over my head.

– Just open your mind – Paul sent. – Try not to think of anything. Completely clear your head of any thoughts. Empty your brain –

– Maybe you should be the one with the pillowcase on your head –

– Are you gonna shut up or what? –

I sighed. I lay on my back. I let myself relax. My arms were by my sides, with the palms of my hands resting flat on the carpet. I felt

106

ridiculous and hoped nobody would come home and see me like this; I could just imagine what my brother would have to say if he saw me.

– Concentrate – Paul told me.

It's actually very difficult to empty your mind. To do it completely I had to think about what I was emptying it of. Telephone numbers, song lyrics, faces of people at school, and the time my father told me off for not feeding the hamster, all bubbled up through the pool of my memory but were quick to burst and evaporate. I found the more I relaxed the easier it became. I let myself breathe deeply. I felt the little bubbles pop and burst as they reached the surface.

I didn't think about where I was or what I was doing. I didn't think about the feel of the carpet below me or the sound of my breathing.

I stared at the blackness in front of my eyes. I concentrated on that blackness, emptiness, nothingness. And I could feel it working. I could feel it wrapping itself, around me. But I didn't let myself think about it working, I let the empty blackness carry me away with it. Black velvet swaddling clothes. Bundling me up. I didn't imagine shadows or folds, simply the dark. I let it envelop me completely and absolutely.

Then the pain in my hand started. It started slow, nagging, and spread the hurt into my whole arm. I didn't really notice it at first. To notice it I would have had to think about it, and right then I wasn't thinking about a single thing. It was like sleeping, but without the dreams. There was something so safe about being absolutely nowhere, about being absolutely nothing. An intoxicating safety. And possibly an illusory safety.

The hurt in my hand scratched a chink of light in the blackness.

My mind made a grab for it. Thoughts rushed in. And that was when the pain suddenly flared.

Instant, hot, shocking. I think I cried out. I may have screamed. I ripped the pillowcase off my head and the pain disappeared as immediately as it had appeared. But a slim line of blood ran across my palm from the old cut.

– Paul? –

He didn't answer me.

– Are you all right, Paul? –

– Er, yeah, I think so – He was quiet again. I waited for him to say something else. And he made me wait for quite a while before he sent: – I'm bleeding –

I looked at my own hand. The thin trail of blood ran from the wound, twisting around the contours of my palm to the ball of my thumb and then down to my wrist. I wondered if the cut would ever heal properly.

– What's your blood look like? – I asked.

– What d'you mean? –

I felt embarrassed. – Oh, nothing. Doesn't matter –

– I felt something – Paul told me. – I saw something too, I think –

– What? –

He sent me a mental shrug. – I don't know. It's a bit hard to explain. Did you feel anything? –

– Sort of – I sent, wondering whether feeling nothing could actually be classed as feeling something. Then: – Look, I'm not sure whether we should really be doing this kind of thing, you know. It seems a bit . . . well, a bit out of our league really –

I was surprised when Paul agreed. – Yeah – he sent. – I know what you mean. I don't know what happened, but it sure freaked the hell out of me – He was laughing now. As ever, he hadn't been knocked off stride for long. – I mean, it's scary enough just listening to your normal thoughts, who says I really want to listen to anything else you might have running around your head –

I knew he was making a joke of something that hadn't gone exactly as he'd wanted it to. It made me think that he was a little more shaken than he was willing to let on.

Chapter Eleven

Neither Paul nor I had mentioned what had happened earlier that day. Not that we were avoiding the subject or anything, it was just that for Paul something more important had come along to occupy his mind, namely having a good time. And for me I'd simply filed it away as yet one more tick to occasionally nag at my mind. I was quite proud of my filing system, it was certainly becoming something of a skill. And anyway, my hand had stopped bleeding within a few minutes, the ache in it had subsided even quicker, so I'd kind of told myself that there was really nothing to worry about.

I'd taken a leaf out of Paul's book and let my mind become occupied with other things. After all, it had been a full two weeks since we'd become blood brothers and a whole week since I'd come to accept the power and use it. So you can understand why I was beginning to think that Fridays were symbolic somehow. And although I didn't want tonight to be an exception, I was rather hoping it was going to be exceptional in some way.

– One coming your way – Paul sent. – Blonde, tall, black dress. She's with another lass with silly hair –

– I see her – The girl in question made her way past me and stood talking with her mate over to my left, leaning against the cigarette machine. The mate's hair was short and spikey, kind of red, but closer to orange, and covered in so much gel it looked plastic. The taller girl with blonde hair was pale and pretty. The black dress did wonders with her slim figure. – Nice – I sent.

– Very nice – Paul expanded. – She with anyone except that other lass? –

– Not by the looks of it –

– Okay – he sent. – That's another one to keep in mind for later –

– And I suppose I have to put up with the mate with silly hair, do I? –

Paul chuckled inside my head. – I just thought she was more your type –

We had set up positions on opposite sides of the nightclub. Paul was hanging around near the bar and I was sitting on a stool with my back to the DJ's box. We couldn't see each other from our separate positions, but between us we had virtually the whole of the club covered.

– What d'you think of this one then? – Paul asked.

– Which one? –

– She's coming around the side of the dance floor. Short skirt. Kinky boots –

– Can't see her –

– Black curly hair. She's on her own –

I spotted the girl he was talking about. She moved to stand with her back to me at the edge of the dance floor. – All right I suppose – I sent.

Paul tutted at me. – Don't be so picky. This is Swift's remember. You can't be too choosy in here –

The club had originally been called Shades. And before it had become known as Swift's, before I'd ever been old enough to come here, it had gone under such epithets as Glam, Jasper's and Hot Nite Venue, all dependent on the discernment of the proprieter at the time. The nightclub itself sat above The Royal Bank of Scotland on Gulliver Street and the only entrance was through a tiny doorway and up some narrow, dimly-lit stairs. Over the years the doorway had become affectionately known as The Minging Doorway, but nobody had ever found anything affectionate to say about the stairs. Mainly because if the bouncers ever threw you out it was down them that you fell. Not that Paul and I had ever been thrown out of course, although we had dodged the odd flying body or two in our time.

Once inside you realised it was everything that The Minging Doorway and the dark, narrow stairs had promised it would be. Swift's was only a small club, but usually full. Mainly of students. Your feet stuck to the carpet if you remained in the same place for too long, the windows along the back wall were propped open with coat hangers and it was usually too dark in there to notice the stains on the wall-paper, unless you were being particularly finicky. This was probably because the club didn't have much in the way of disco lighting (one green light, one red) so to try and compensate the DJ often threw the dance floor into complete darkness. Which, it could be argued, helped add to the atmosphere during slow songs, but then again only increased the danger during the more up-tempo numbers.

Tonight the club wasn't as full as we'd often seen it in the past. Probably because the students had all gone home for the summer, and those that came back to Cleeston at the end of every term had already been back for a few weeks. The DJ still made sure the dance floor was chocker though, and in places like this the bar area is seldom ever empty.

I think people go to nightclubs because they're basically like parties that you're always invited to, every weekend. They're not as good as proper parties admittedly, mainly because they're not as inti-mate. But they're better than parties for that exact same reason; you never know just who's going to appear in a nightclub. And that's why I liked them. For me they've always held a kind of romantic appeal. Nightclubs are the kind of places where you dream of love at first sight ('we locked eyes across a crowded room . . .' etc). Maybe not as much as you do at airports or train stations, admittedly. But the notion is still there.

I watched the girl with the short skirt and kinky boots. She watched the dancers on the dance floor, resting her weight on one leg, her bum slightly off-centre inside her denim skirt. She was drinking Diamond

White straight out of the bottle. My dad had always claimed to dislike seeing women drinking straight out of the bottle, although it was something that had never bothered me. Maybe it was the generation gap? She ran a hand through her dark, curly hair, and flicked it away from her neck as if it irritated her. She turned to take a look around herself; her tight, white T-shirt glowed under the fluorescent lights. Her breasts looked just about Wonderbra'd to death. She was definitely attractive, but only in an obvious kind of way.

– Sorry, Paul. She's just not my type –

– Not your type? What d'you mean, not your type? So you've got a *type* now, have you? – He laughed. – I've never known you to be fussy before. You always said that as long as they washed regularly and didn't listen to Robson and Jerome you'd be more than happy –

– No, Paul. That was you –

– Oh, right, yeah, so it was – he chuckled. – You don't mind if I add her to my list then, do you? –

– Not at all, go for your life –

– That's great. Cheers – He paused for a moment. – You know, if all of these work out for me tonight – he sent, – I'm gonna be one hell of a busy guy –

– I believe it – I imagined him smoothing the material of his Magical Pulling pants and had to laugh.

The place was beginning to fill up slightly and the dance floor had started to spill over. I looked at my watch. 11:15; the pubs were kicking out. The DJ had also noticed the sudden influx of bodies and the music was cranked that little bit higher, the record swapped for something a little more up-tempo, and the dance floor heaved. Now hopefully I'd be able to add a couple more to my list, because it certainly seemed to be lacking somewhat when you compared it to Paul's. I wondered if I really was being too fussy . . . I decided to take a wander as far as the toilets, to see if there was anything interesting along the way, anything that caught my eye.

There was one girl in leather pants, red T-shirt with a big white heart on the front. She was dancing with marvellous swinging movements of her hips and backside. Great body, I thought, but a rather peculiar face. It was really pointy, a big wedge of a nose and eyes spaced wide enough apart to make it look as though they were on either side of her head. I decided she looked too much like a lizard and therefore not my type either.

But the girl with the ponytail looked as though she was good fun. She was sitting at one of the few tables talking to a group of friends who were huddled round. She was waving her hands excitedly, laughing. The group of friends laughed when she did, waved their hands when she did, all caught up in whatever tale she was telling. But when she stood up I realised that she was probably too tall for me. I'd had a phobia about tall women ever since Mrs Finch in the Junior School. Scary lady.

So what about the coloured girl in the purple dress? She looked very pretty. Very pretty indeed. She also looked very taken when some short guy in a T-shirt three sizes too big for him came up and started sucking on her face. I recognised him as Dave Games from last year's upper-sixth. He'd always been lucky with the women.

115

I had to queue in the gents. I looked at the condom machine hanging next to the smeared mirror with a feeling a little too close to longing for comfort. Too fussy; I had to be, that just had to be the problem. Maybe a girl who looked like a lizard wouldn't be so bad. I mean, if her lizardy features spread all the way to her tongue she'd make a great kisser. And this thing about tall women, it was positively ridiculous. Surely not all women over six foot enjoyed crushing ladybirds between finger and thumb as they told you off for not doing your homework.

I managed to chase three fag butts down the drain, equalling my previous record, but it didn't make me feel any better. Okay, so I felt immortal. Okay, so Paul and I had this amazing power . . . Okay, but I hadn't kissed a girl in ages. It felt as though it was the only thing missing from my life, the only thing that was stopping me from making this summer the best yet.

I stepped out of the brightly-lit toilets and back into the semi-darkness of the club. I realised how chilly the gents had been when the heat of people rolled over me. I pushed my misty glasses up my nose and headed back towards the dance floor. I told myself that if there were enough people crammed into this place to raise the temperature then there surely must be someone for me somewhere. My problem was that I wanted to meet a woman who would not only catch my eye, but who would also make me catch my breath. And somehow I didn't think there were many of them about.

But then there she was.

She was dancing. She had fair hair that fell to just below her chin, kind of bobbed. She was wearing a tight, black, ribbed-effect T-shirt that didn't quite tuck into the top of her jeans. Every time she raised her hands above her head as she danced I could see her belly. She had a wonderful smile, but it wasn't aimed at me. It flashed by me briefly to land on some guy in a tartan shirt. And he was quick to make his move, squeezing, elbowing himself a bit of room on the dance floor. He received a few shoves and even more dirty looks from the other already-cramped dancers but I didn't blame him for not wanting to give up that wonderful smile. The last girl I could remember who'd had a smile like that had been at Matty Harker's party . . .

And that thought stopped me in my tracks.

Could it be . . .?

– Paul! Paul! –

– Yeah? What? Somebody nice? –

– It's her! –

– Straight up? – he sent. – Is it? Really? –

– Yeah, yeah, it is. It has to be. I swear it is –

– It can't be –

– It is. I'm telling you, it's her. It really is –

– Well I'll be – Paul sent. – Who'd've guessed it – He paused for a moment. – So who're we talking about then? –

– The girl with the Gameboy – I was getting all excited. – Matty's sister. Katie Harker –

– Well, you don't hear that name everyday – he told me.

I took a couple of steps away from the dance floor, faded myself into the crowd slightly, moving back against the wall, and watched her. Mixed emotions bubbled to the surface in my head. Maybe that squirming feeling of embarrassment after our last meeting should have been stronger, but seeing her like this reminded me of just how beautiful she was. The smile was so wide and open. Her golden hair. The coloured lights above the dance floor flashed and changed, flashed and changed, and I swear I saw the jewel in her nose give off the tiniest of sparkles. I looked at her feet, and her cherry-red DMs. She laughed, dancing close with the guy in the tartan shirt. And I hated him, whoever the hell he thought he was.

I wanted to talk to her. I wanted to go and elbow my way onto the dance floor like the other guy had. But did I have the guts to do it? Would she recognise me? And what would her memories of me be like if she did? I ran my fingers along my newly-replenished eyebrows.

I stood leaning, watching her, wishing I had the guts to make a move, scared I'd make a fool of myself even if I did.

Paul pushed his way through the crowd towards me. He stood and leaned with me. The song changed again, to something a bit more relaxed this time, but Katie stayed on the dance floor. A circle of three of four lads had formed around her, Mr Tartan Shirt was only one of a group now.

– You gonna to talk to her then? – Paul asked.

I shrugged. – Not yet. I haven't worked out what to say –

– So what? Why don't we just get on the dance floor and catch her eye? I'm sure she'll remember us –

– Look, let me do it my own way, okay? –

It was Paul's turn to shrug. – If that's what you want –

– It is –

– Good –

– Great –

We stood watching her a little while longer, then Paul sent: – I just know what you're like, that's all – he told me. – I mean, we might as well go home now. There's no point hanging around if we both know how it's gonna turn out. You're just gonna stand here all night, watching her, wishing you had the guts to make a move, scared you'll make a fool of yourself even if you did –

I turned and looked him in the eyes. – I hate you –

He smirked at me.

I ignored him. I always did when he was right. I watched Katie being watched by the men surrounding her on the dance floor. She smiled at the ones who caught her eye. It was as though she were collecting their stares like tokens, like petrol coupons she could exchange for a prize later on in the evening. And obviously the more she collected the more special the prize would be.

– Paul? –

– Yeah? –

– This may sound a bit funny, but would you say that I was special in some way or other? – I asked.

He laughed dryly inside my head. – Let me get this straight – he began. – You're standing there using the power of telepathy . . . You're standing there using the paranormal to communicate with me . . . You're standing there using a supernatural occurrence to ask me

119

whether or not I think you're special in some way or other? Is that right? –

I grinned at him. – Something like that – I sent, pushing myself off the wall and weaving my way in between the people hovering around the edge of the dance floor.

She saw me coming and I almost lost it. Her big and beautiful eyes slid right over me at first, and I nearly turned one-eighty to go and stand with Paul again. But they came back, recognition widened them, and she smiled at me. I smiled in return. And I admit it may have been a little nervous, but it sure as hell wasn't lopsided. It didn't slip. It stayed there as she moved away from Mr Tartan Shirt and chums to dance with me.

– Go Chris, go! Go Chris, Go! – Paul was a cheerleader inside my head.

Now, the old me, the not-so-special me would have stumbled at this point for sure. Self-consciousness would have sneaked up from behind and thrown my legs into a rhythmical turmoil. But this was the new me, the special me, and this me had feet that worked. Not as well as they could have done admittedly, so I wiggled the top half of my body that little bit extra to compensate. And it seemed to work. So I did it some more. Even the DJ was on my side. Not only was the next song he played an old Oasis number, one I knew well, but he also kept switching the lights off for long periods at a time so Katie couldn't see me anyway. And I made the most of it. I wasn't exactly dancing for my life, nothing quite so melodramatic, but I certainly felt as though I had a point to prove.

– Two, four, six, eight, who do we appreciate? – Paul chanted.

Have you seen *Pulp Fiction?* That bit when John Travolta and Uma Thurman are dancing in Jackrabbit Slim's? That was us. Me and Katie.

– Gimme a 'c', gimme an 'h', gimme an 'r' . . . –

Katie's smile was on full beam. And on me. It was obvious I wasn't the world's greatest dancer, but it was just as obvious I didn't care. It was a funky-twisting-shaky thing I was doing, with Paul cheering and applauding inside my head. I felt as if I were back in my rightful place again: on top of the world. Mr Tartan Shirt tried to push his bad dress sense in our way, but Katie wouldn't even glance at him as she oh-so-easily side-stepped around him. He then tried to jostle me, but I certainly wasn't going to move, no way, and the poor sap had to admit defeat.

There was a tiny hitch when Oasis came to an end only to be replaced by a song I didn't recognise. A twinge of panic needled at me and I found myself turning to Paul for help. Luckily it only lasted for a second or two.

'I love this song,' Katie told me.

– I love this DJ – I told Paul.

It wasn't the drink, I'd only had one bottle of Newcastle Brown. It wasn't the song either, I've already told you I'd never heard it before. So I guess it could have been the atmosphere . . . But I'd really like to think it was Katie who was making me grin from ear to ear.

The song came to an end. There was a slight, few seconds pause while the DJ fought to cue-up the next record. Katie and I looked at each other expectantly, then groaned in unison when some terrible seventies disco tune squeezed itself out of the speakers.

Katie grabbed my hand. 'Come on,' she said. 'Let's get a drink.'

I turned and grinned at Paul.

– Steady . . . –

– . . . Progress –

My grin slipped a little when Mr Tartan Shirt came over to talk to Katie, then grew as huge as ever when he stormed off. I don't know what she'd said to him, but he sure as hell wasn't happy. He wouldn't even look at me, he just pushed roughly past and headed towards the toilets. I didn't care, Katie was with *me* now. Even though I hadn't said one word to her yet, there was a kind of understanding as she led me towards the bar that we were now officially together for the evening. It made me feel great. And she looked great. There was a huge balloon of promise and expectation growing in my gut.

Unfortunately it only took one little prick to burst it. Well, he was quite a big prick really. Bigger than me anyway. Bigger than most in fact.

– Ask her who she's with. Ask her if she's got a mate for me –

I ignored him. Instead I said: 'I wasn't sure if you'd remember me.'

'Of course I do,' she said. 'And I'm really sorry about that night. I can't believe I threw you out of the bathroom when you were feeling so ill. I'm really, really sorry. I'm not usually so nasty,' she told me.

'I trust you,' I said.

And she smiled. 'I'm sure there's plenty who wouldn't.'

We were having to queue for our drinks. I was wondering whether or not I should offer to pay for Katie's. It was the kind of thing my father had always told me to do, but in these politically correct times of ours I knew how insulted some women could get with the merest hint of male domination.

– Dump her now if she's a feminist – Paul advised me.

'I bet you felt dreadful the next day.'

I nodded. 'Rough as a badger's bum,' I admitted. 'I mean, really, *really* bad. I thought I was dying. And nobody cared.'

'I'm sure somebody did,' she said. 'What about your mother? She must have cared.'

I waved my hand derisively. 'Her least of all. She was ready to sit back and watch me die as long as it taught me how to be a more responsible adult.'

'And did it?' she asked.

'Oh yeah. Definitely,' I said. 'Well, maybe. Sort of.' I grinned sheepishly. 'It depends on how you look at it really.'

Katie laughed, the sound the perfect partner for her smile.

'And I'm not sure if you noticed,' I whispered in mock secrecy, 'but unfortunately I wasn't exactly *all there* that night.'

She looked a little confused. 'I'm sorry?'

I leaned in close to her ear. 'My eyebrows. They'd been kidnapped.'

She laughed again, twigging on. 'You couldn't tell,' she lied.

'Thank you,' I said with a sarcastic grin.

Things were going well. The conversation was rolling. Because there were so many people clammering around the bar we were pushed up close to each other. All I had to do was raise my right hand an inch or two and it would be touching the bare flesh of her belly where her crop top had left it exposed.

We steadily made progress towards the front of the disjointed queue, and with all the pushing and jostling I'd somehow been forced in front of her. Which I reckoned was quite lucky because now I could offer her a drink and not look as though I was trying to force some clichéd gentlemanliness on her.

'What can I get you?' I asked.

'Bacardi and Coke, please,' she said, without offering me any money to pay for it.

I turned to the barman. 'Bottle of Brown and . . .' The words kind of stuck. I think my mouth continued to move for a bit, but the words 'Bacardi and Coke' had been lost for the time being. From the other side of the bar Bob Moody's mate, St. Pierre, stared back at me.

He had his hands planted firmly on either side of the Guinness pump. He seemed to loom over that bar at me. His shoulders were wide enough to block out my view of the bottle fridge behind him. His pockmarked face looked a cadaverous grey in the fluorescent tube light. The fluorescent tube light which winked, flickered, flashing above his head, reminding me of lightning strikes on a stormy night. All he needed, I realised, was a couple of bolts through his neck and I would have been ordering my drinks from Frankenstein's barman. We both remembered our last encounter all too well. He was wearing a white shirt with the sleeves rolled up past his elbows and I caught my eyes travelling up and down his bare forearms looking for bruising. He also caught my eyes doing it and growled at me. I mean it. He actually, truly, physically growled at me.

He stood up straight, like an eclipse, and turned his back on me to fetch a Newcastle Brown from the fridge. He took the bottle to the end of the bar where the bottle opener was screwed to the wall. He popped the cap. But instead of letting it fall into the bin below he caught it in his massive hand, then dropped it to clatter on the tiled floor at his feet. He never took his eyes off me. He crouched to pick up the cap and, whilst he was out of view of the other people around the bar, he puckered up his lips and pushed a slow, thick trail of saliva from between those lips into the neck of the bottle. He stood up slowly, flicked the cap in to the bin, and put the Newcastle Brown down on to the bar in front of me. I could see a single, solitary spit bubble on the bottle's rim. I could only imagine what was slithering its way down the inside of the glass neck.

'Anything else?' he asked.

'Bacardi and Coke,' I whimpered.

I prayed he wouldn't do anything to Katie's drink. I watched him slowly, laboriously pour it. He was letting me sweat, but luckily the drink arrived next to the bottle of Brown in front of me untainted.

He took my money and when he returned my change (which was 50p short, not that I said anything) he whispered, 'Bob's meeting me when I get off.' I turned to retreat with the drinks. 'Maybe we'll see you and your mate later,' he added.

Katie and I headed back over towards Paul. 'Did you know him?' Katie asked.

'Sort of,' I answered. 'I didn't know he worked here, though.'

'He's big isn't he?'

I nodded. 'Very.'

Paul was still standing where I'd left him. I shouted introductions over the music. Katie said she recognised him from the party and asked if his girlfriend was here tonight as well and Paul explained as subtly as he could that Jane Lois-Lane wasn't actually his girlfriend. He didn't explain, however, that she was someone else's girlfriend, and that was the part that was troubling me at the time.

'So, don't I get a drink, then?' Paul asked, staring at the bottle of Brown I was carrying.

'Eh?' I hadn't heard him, he'd knocked me off my train of thought, I'd been too busy wondering exactly what I should do.

He raised his voice to match the volume of the music. 'I said, couldn't you be bothered to buy me a drink? We've got to share now, have we?' He took the bottle from out of my hands. He'd grabbed it before I could stop him.

I stared at it in his hand. 'Oh, sorry. I didn't think.'

'Some mate you are.' He shook his head, winking at Katie. He was putting on a performance for her sake. He lifted the bottle up to his face, and squinted at the label. 'And you know I hate Newcy Brown,' he said, tutting, handing me the bottle back.

I squinted at the label myself. I decided I'd rather gone off Newcastle Brown too, and put it down on a table behind me.

I looked at Katie, who was swaying to the music, mouthing the lyrics of the song (the Levellers, I think). She smiled her wonderful smile at me. I smiled back, then took Paul to one side. I didn't exactly need to, but it seemed to add weight to the situation.

– We've got a problem –

– Yeah? What's that? – he asked nonchalantly. His eyes were on a couple of girls on the dance floor.

– St. Pierre's here – I told him.

His eyes met mine. – St. Pierre? –

I nodded.

Paul's eyes scanned the faces in the crowd. – Where is he? –

– He's working behind the bar – I sent. – I didn't know he worked here –

Paul shook his head. – Me neither. Is Bob Moody here, too? –

– No, but St. Pierre reckons he's coming to meet him after work –

– We'd better get going then –

– What d'you mean? –

– Well, I certainly don't want to be around when Bob Moody shows up – Paul sent. – I don't think I'm top of his party list somehow, do you? –

He was already beginning to walk away, heading for the cloakroom.

– I can't go, Paul. Not yet –

– Why not? –

– Katie –

We both turned to look at her. She saw us and stepped over.

127

'You're looking serious all of a sudden,' she said. She took hold of my hand. 'Come and dance with me, that'll cheer you up.'

– Come on, Paul. Don't make me leave. Not now –

– If we go now – Paul sent, – we'll be able to get in somewhere else and find some other lasses. One each –

– I don't want another lass –

– Yeah, but do you want your face rearranged by Bob Moody? –

– Not particularly –

– Well then. Let's go –

– But Bob Moody's not after me –

– St..Pierre is. He's gonna want to kick you around a bit after you belted him with that steering lock –

I shrugged. – Maybe –

– But you're willing to risk it all for the love of a beautiful woman? – Paul sent sarcastically.

I shrugged again. – Maybe – I repeated.

– Oh, come on! – He threw his hands in the air dramatically. – I was taking the mick, for Christ's sake – He grabbed me by the shoulders. – Don't do this to me, Chris. We've got to go. You know what Bob Moody and St. Pierre're like. They're not gonna stop kicking me until I've got nothing left to kick –

I shook my head. – I . . . –

'Is everything all right?' Katie asked.

Paul and I suddenly looked at her. She was watching us with a frown on her face. It put lines in her forehead and little crinkles at the top of her nose. (Did I tell you how beautiful she was?) I realised that it must look rather strange to her, and to anybody else watching for that matter, the way Paul and I were carrying on. Neither of us were speaking, neither of us were even opening our mouths, but we were shrugging, nodding, throwing our hands in the air . . .

'Er, yeah. Everything's fine,' I said. 'Isn't it Paul?'

Paul nodded. 'Yeah. Fine.' He nodded his head a little too vigorously. 'No problem.'

She wasn't sure whether to believe us or not. Her head was cocked on one side. But she said: 'You're mad. The pair of you.' And started laughing.

Paul and I laughed along with her, albeit rather awkwardly. Then followed her reluctantly on to the dance floor, and danced even more awkwardly. I seemed to have lost my funk and been deserted by my shake. Luckily I don't think Katie noticed.

– As soon as this song finishes – Paul told me, – I'm going –

I didn't answer.

Paul danced his way in front of me. – Are you coming or what? –

– What about Katie? –

– Just get her phone number or something –

Again I was silent. I knew Paul could easily go on his own, I'd even give him the money for a taxi home if he wanted me to. But it would somehow be like deserting him. Leaving the other for a woman was something neither of us had ever done. It had always been like some unspoken rule; friends came first. And I guessed it was even more poignant now we were blood brothers and were sharing what we did, but . . . I looked at Katie. The eyes, the smile, the glimpses of her belly. Let's be honest, somebody like her didn't talk to me every day of the week. I looked back at Paul. He was my blood brother. It was obvious he was worried. He wanted to get going as soon as he possibly could. But it was all his own fault.

– Okay – I sent, reluctantly. – I'll get her number –

The song finished and I led Katie off the dance floor. I made up some rubbishy excuse about why we had to leave early. I think she bought it.

'I'm really sorry,' I said. 'It's Paul's mum, you see. She's . . . Well, you know what I mean.'

Katie nodded. 'I understand.' I couldn't work out exactly how upset she was about me leaving.

'Why don't you come with us?'

'Oh, no, that's okay. I've got plenty of friends here,' she said.

This gave me terrible visions of Mr Tartan Shirt. I'd seen him hanging around in the crowd ever since we'd come back from the bar, on the prowl, waiting to pounce. 'I promise I'll ring you soon,' I said.

'I promise I'll answer,' she told me. But I couldn't help feeling that I'd just missed out on the opportunity of a lifetime.

My head was hanging low when Paul and I went to get our coats from the cloakroom. He tried to put an arm around my shoulders but I threw it off viciously.

He shrugged. He knew I was angry. – So, where to now? – he asked tentatively.

– Home –

– Home? It's only just twelve, and my pants haven't even begun to get warmed-up yet. We'll still get in somewhere else if we're lucky –

– I don't feel lucky any more – I told him. – I just want to go home –

– Oh, come on, don't be like that. You got her phone number didn't you? –

I didn't answer. I could tell he was feeling bad, he wasn't so inconsiderate that he didn't feel slightly responsible for my bad mood. But I could feel one of his jokes coming, I could see him out of the corner of my eye building up to some pathetic punch line or other, some weak gag that was aimed at making me feel better. Well, not this time, I told myself. No way. I wasn't going to let him get away with it this time.

– Don't even try –

He looked rather taken aback. – What? Don't try what? –

I pushed past him, shouldering on my coat, heading down the dark stairs. – Don't lay any of your naff jokes on me because I really don't want to hear them –

– Hey, don't blame me if you're in a bad mood –

I stopped on the stairs and glared at him. – What the hell d'you mean, don't blame you? I'd be up there dancing with the girl of my dreams if it wasn't for you – I almost punched him, but somehow managed to restrain myself. – If maybe you could keep your hands on your own girlfriend and off other people's then maybe I could find a girlfriend of *my* own –

– I haven't got a girlfriend –

– No reason to mess around with someone else's – I started back down the stairs and headed on outside, looking for a taxi. – You've got a total lack of responsibility –

Paul shrugged. – Responsibility? – he asked. – I've done puberty, I've done adolescence. So when's responsibility start? –

I ignored him. I stalked away down the street.

– I don't know what all this fuss about girlfriends is anyway – he mumbled inside my head. – Everybody's so concerned with getting a girlfriend, and they're nothing special. I mean, what's a girlfriend? If you ask me, they're just crap mates who let you snog them, that's all –

That was it. That was the punch line he'd been working up to all this time.

I didn't laugh.

– Help! Help! There's something in my bed –

– Leave me alone. I'm trying to sleep –

– Arrgh! It's on my leg, it's crawling up my leg –

– I mean it, Paul. You've pushed me far enough for one night –

– It's . . . it's huge. I've never seen a snake this big before. It's a monster! –

– For God's sake, Paul, just shut up, will you! –

– Oh, my mistake, it's not a snake after all, hee hee hee –

PART FOUR

Chapter Twelve

So there I was, the thought of what my parents were going to say flashing through my mind and this fat farmer's hand on my shoulder. And there was Paul, legging it across the open field, startling the cows. I watched him go. I watched him dive through the hedge that bordered the road, and disappear.

The farmer was swearing at me, and yanked me away from the barbed wire. He'd let go of my shoulder but had now grabbed my arm just above my elbow. His grip was tight and painful.

'. . . thinking you can come on private property all the time, acting like hooligans, I don't know what they teach you in schools these days. And your parents are just as bad. Well, we'll just have to tell them straight about this one, won't we? I'm not standing for any more of this . . .'

I was marched along the inside of the barbed wire, away from the road. The farmer viciously swatted branches out of his path, tramping down nettles and tall grass in his big rubber boots. The smell of cow-dung clung to him. The sun was so very hot and I was sweating. He wouldn't slacken the grip he had on me. I could see no way out; the spiteful fence to my right, the thick, tangled bushes on my left, yet he wouldn't slacken his grip. I stumbled slightly but he dragged me on.

'. . . not like this in my day. We had respect for our elders . . .'

He suddenly pulled me away from the fence and into the bushes through a well-used gap. There was a narrow, two-plank bridge over the deep ditch and he hauled me across it. He hadn't stopped cursing me yet. He led the way out through the bushes on the other side and up a short slope into an open field. I could see the white farmhouse across the field, his tractor parked on the dirt track outside.

I looked over my shoulder. I searched the bushes for a face. I didn't think Paul would really leave me. Not Paul. We were best friends. I reckoned he'd be concocting some kind of escape plan or other. He wouldn't leave me to get done by myself.

But the fields and bushes were empty.

If he suddenly appears, I told myself, it will give me a chance to wrench my arm free. The farmer would be startled and it should only take a good hard yank. I reckoned that once I was free I'd be able to outrun him quite easily. I'd be on the road and away before he'd even realised what was happening. Or maybe, I thought, maybe I could trip him up. I watched the way he waddled in his heavy galoshes. It would be as simple as sticking my foot out and then watching him tumble; he'd have to let go of me to save his fall.

' . . . buckle of his belt is what my father'd use on us. And we'd never step out of line again, that was for sure . . .'

The farmhouse was looming closer and closer. If I was going to try and run then I had to do it now. Either that or trip him up. But I didn't do either. I was a scared thirteen-year-old who'd been caught red-handed. And Paul was nowhere to be seen. I started inventing excuses. My mum and dad were going to hit the roof when this fat farmer phoned them up.

I wasn't taken to the farmhouse however; the old man had different plans for me. I was escorted past the tractor and through a wide, unlocked gate that led into a large, open yard behind the farmhouse. There were two huge, hangar-like barns and another tractor with a trailer full of hay hooked up to it. The farmer dragged me across the yard, past the first barn; its massive doors were wide open and inside it was full of heavy farm equipment, all painted red. The second barn's doors were closed and padlocked, but there was a smaller wooden door set into the bigger one. The farmer drew back the bolt and I was pushed inside. It was dark in there, barns don't have windows, and it smelled as bad as he did. Loose hay covered the floor; bales of the stuff were piled high up the sides.

'I don't want your sort in my house,' the old man snarled. 'What I want is to tie you up in here, like the animal you are.' His face was pushed close to mine, red and bloated with anger. He had patches of dirty-grey stubble on his chin and cheeks. He was squeezing my arm hard enough to bring tears to my eyes, but I wasn't going to cry, no way, because that was exactly what he wanted me to do. We hadn't been doing any harm, he never used the ditch anyway, what good was it to him? I'd cry in front of my parents when they got here, but there was no way I was going to cry in front of him.

'It's the police I'm phoning,' he told me. 'Not your mam and dad. Because the police'll do something about it. Lock you up proper.' He gave my arm one last, hard squeeze for luck then left me alone in the dark, smelly barn. He slammed the door closed and I heard the bolt thunk into place.

And that was when the tears came. But I brushed them away hastily. No fat farmer was going to scare me, get me into trouble, make me cry.

I was on my feet and searching for a way out. There had to be a crack or a gap somewhere in the massive wooden walls.

I started digging at the stacked up bales of hay. I managed to squeeze in between them and the wall. I squirmed my way along, pushing against them to tip them away and leave enough room for me to move. The wood was slatted and overlapping. I tried to get a good enough grip to rip at the slats, forcing my fingers in between to prise them apart. But it was no use, I was nowhere near strong enough. The straw pricked me through my T-shirt and scratched my bare arms. The bales were heavy and it wasn't long before I was sweating and quickly beginning to realise I was fighting a losing battle. To be able to get to the walls all the way at the back of the barn I would have to move bales that were stacked seven and eight high and at least three wide. And how long could a phone call to the police possibly take?

My mind flipped through ideas for escape like a train timetable flips through possible destinations and arrival times. Because I simply had to escape, there was no doubt about that. I stood in the centre of the huge building, spinning around, my eyes searching for something, anything. It seemed like the biggest prison cell in the world, but the darkness and the smell closed the walls in on me, made it all seem so claustrophobic. I climbed the bales of hay to the very top, until I had to duck my head because of the roof. I struggled to kick a couple of bales from underneath me and they tumbled to smash and burst silently on the hard floor. Maybe if Paul was here to help . . .?

But Paul had run away and left me.

There was a hollow, sickly feeling in my stomach. I was so frightened I was beginning to feel ill. I had to sit down to ease the nausea.

Maybe if I hid somewhere, I told myself. If I could get myself hidden behind some of the larger stacks or buried in the middle somewhere the farmer would never be able to find me. Or I could maybe hide behind the door and make a run for it when he came in; I'd be halfway back across the fields before he even knew what had happened. Or if I could find a big stick I could knock him out when he unbolted the door. I'd seen it done loads of times in the movies.

Where was Paul? I couldn't believe he'd just left me to get caught. He'd run away and left me here, left me to face this alone. I'd seen him legging it across the field. What should I say when the police asked me who he was? Should I sprag on him? But I was going to get out of here before the police turned up. I couldn't let the police catch me. My dad was going to explode if the police took me home.

I stood up again, but the fear that crawled through my stomach was so overwhelming all I could do was sit back down. And the tears soon washed away what little was left of my determination.

Chapter
Thirteen

The guy sitting opposite me on the bus was wearing headphones. I couldn't see the actual Walkman, but the wire from his earplugs ran down outside the front of his jacket to disappear underneath his clothes. For all I knew, and from the way he was sitting, the wire could have eventually led to his penis and he was actually listening to what lustful thoughts it was having this evening.

Now that *would* be a useful invention, I thought to myself.

– What would? –

He startled me, but I tried not to let it show. – Nothing. I wasn't talking to you –

– Oh, go on. Tell me –

– I said, I wasn't talking to you –

– Suit yourself – he sent, sounding more than a little put out. – Just don't think so loudly next time –

I couldn't understand why Paul had heard me, I hadn't meant to send to him. I wondered if he'd always been able to do this, or if he was somehow becoming more adept at using the power than me. I didn't like the idea of what he'd just done. It meant that not only could he invade my mind with his thoughts whenever he wanted to, but he could also pick up on any loose thoughts of mine that were flying around out there. And my private thoughts were only meant for me, not him, nor anybody else. They were my thoughts. Mine.

– You haven't been in touch today – he told me.

– No, I know –

– I tried to get in touch with you –

– Did you? When was that? –

– Once this morning and twice this afternoon. Didn't you hear me? –

– No – I lied.

– You must have been busy – He knew I was lying. – You must have had other things on your mind – He laughed half-heartedly.

I didn't even try, and an uncomfortable silence stretched out between us. The bus slowly jogged me along towards town. It felt kind of childish to be holding this grudge against Paul because of what had happened at Swift's last night, but I simply wasn't able to shake it off. And to tell the truth, I didn't think I really wanted to.

– Are you coming to see me tonight? – he asked.

– No – I replied. – I'm going out –

– Oh yeah? – he sent. – Where're you going? – He was trying so hard to sound light-hearted, he was desperate to smooth things over.

– Just out –

– You're seeing Katie, aren't you? You phoned her and she's agreed to go out with you. She has, hasn't she? – He was laughing. – Go on, tell the truth, you dirty dog you –

– So what if she has? – I wouldn't let him in. I wouldn't give him an inch.

– Well, that means you didn't balls it up last night, doesn't it? – he told me cheerfully. – So, where're you taking her then? –

– What do you mean, *I* didn't balls it up? –

– Well, it didn't matter that you abandoned her at Swift's, did it? I told you it'd be okay –

– If you remember rightly, it wasn't me who abandoned her – I let him hear my anger. – If you remember rightly, it was you who forced me into leaving her. *If* you remember rightly.

– Ah, well. It was all part of the plan, you see? – he sent. – Treat 'em mean, keep 'em keen. That's what my granny always said –

He simply couldn't see how much he'd upset me. He'd nearly ruined my chances with the woman of my dreams and he really didn't give a damn.

– I don't believe you . . . –

– No, it's true – he told me. – That's why she always had the men at bingo chasing her. They used to bring her flowers and chocolates and all sorts –

I shook my head, counted to ten. Did he know how much he was winding me up?

– Paul? –

– Hey, she's not bringing Matty, is she? That'll certainly add a touch of exuberance to the evening –

– No, he's gone for a drive in his friends' new car apparently –

– Oh, that's a pity – Paul laughed.

– Look, Paul. Will you do me a favour? –

– Anything for you, mate –

– Just get lost, will you? Just leave me alone. Do me this one favour, and don't send to me tonight. Okay? –

– Why not? – He sounded as though his crest had suddenly fallen.

– I don't want you to mess it up for me, that's why –

– I wouldn't –

I wanted to say 'you would', but instead: – Just let me do this one on my own –

– But we've always done everything together –

– Yeah, but I really like Katie. I'm not prepared to risk it –

– You might need me to send you a few of my tried and trusted chat-up lines –

– No, I won't –

– You might say something stupid and need me to get you out of trouble –

– No, Paul –

He tried a little laugh. – You're not even going to send me the gory details? –

– No –

I'd never heard him sound quite so disheartened before. But I reckoned he was putting it on. – Okay then – he sent. – You're the boss – And with that he was gone.

Not that I trusted him of course. I sat still and listened with my mind, blocking out the noise of the bus, waiting to pre-empt him. I was waiting for his punch line.

But it never came.

I could sense myself starting to feel a little worried. But I squashed the thought. I was determined not to feel bad. It was no more than he deserved. Maybe I should have said it a lot sooner.

So I concentrated on the bus journey. I wished it would hurry up. It crawled its way into town, towards the cinema, towards Katie. I looked at the guy sitting opposite me again, the one with the remarkable Walkman. I wondered what he'd have to say if I told him I was on my way to meet the most beautiful girl in the world. I guessed he wouldn't believe me. Cleeston Town wasn't really well known for the winsomeness of its residents. The elephants had a mystical graveyard in the middle of Africa somewhere, and there was a ships' graveyard at the bottom of the ocean. Which meant ugly people had Cleeston. Paul and I had always reckoned they came here to die. But if that guy ever saw her . . . well then he'd just *have* to believe me wouldn't he? And then he'd certainly hear a few choice comments through those ear-plugs of his.

It was a warm evening and she was wearing a pair of blue denim dungarees with a plain white T-shirt underneath. She didn't need a coat. She smiled at me, her eyes so big and wide and beautiful. 'You're late,' she chided. Affectionately I hoped.

I was wearing my favourite shirt, it was a washed-out pale blue with a grandad collar, and my cleanest pair of jeans. I did have smarter clothes, it was just that this particular shirt had always been kind of lucky for me. 'I'm sorry. It was the bus,' I told her. 'My brother nicked the car.' Which was true. And I reckoned he'd done it on purpose. He was better now (too better if you asked me).

She slipped her warm hand into mine. 'So, what are you taking me to see, then?' she asked.

Stupid as it may seem, I hadn't really thought about this. When I'd phoned her earlier I'd only asked her if she wanted to come to the pictures with me, I hadn't even considered what was showing. 'Anything you want.'

She looked at the choice of the three posters behind her. 'Nothing too heavy,' she said. Her head was cocked on one side as she studied them.

'No,' I replied automatically. I hoped I wasn't holding her hand too tightly, I didn't want to squeeze it. But I hoped the grip was firm enough to convey confidence. And I prayed my palm wasn't all sweaty.

She tucked her short, fair hair behind her ear. 'But something with a bit of class. Do you like Robert De Niro?'

'Yeah. Of course.'

'That's settled then.' She grinned at me.

I paid for the tickets and Katie bought us a tub of ice cream each. We walked hand in hand up the stairs to Screen Two and I told myself that if I took her to sit on the back row it would seem a bit tacky. Then again, I obviously didn't want to be sitting right in the middle of everyone else. So we sat about five rows from the back, but over on the far side, and I complemented myself on the compromise. We weren't the only couple in the cinema, in fact the place seemed to be full of them. I guessed it was because a date at the pictures is one of the safest dates going, usually because if you're shy or she's boring there's at least ninety minutes of not having to talk to her. For me and Katie however, I was beginning to hope the film would never come on.

'Try some of mine,' she said. She held out a blob of mucky-coloured ice cream on the end of her tiny plastic spoon.

'What flavour is it?'

'Baileys.'

I shook my head quickly. 'Ugh, no thanks. I'm happy with mine, I've gone off that sort of thing.'

She giggled. 'Because of my brother's party?'

I nodded. 'I'll stick to plain old beer from now on. You can keep your posh stuff, your Southern Comforts and your Baileys'.

'Do you think you can get drunk on it, then?' she asked, turning the small tub around, searching the label.

'I doubt it.'

'Worth a try though,' she laughed, and popped another scoopful into her mouth.

Do you know how I was feeling? Amazing, that's how. We were sitting slouched down low in our seats, our feet up on the backs of the empty chairs in front of us (she was wearing her cherry-reds – I

145

loved those cherry-reds), tucking into our ice cream. I'd never felt so relaxed in the company of a woman before. We talked a lot about school and university. She was telling me that going away was the best thing she'd ever done, that the student's life was a wonderful one. She told me about the people she'd met on her course, and the things they'd got up to.

'Our landlord was such a moron. There were five of us sharing the house and we all hated him. The lock on Sarah's door didn't work properly, the tiles were coming off the walls in the bathroom, and the shower leaked, constantly dripping. And no matter how many times we told him about it, he never came round to fix it. But the thing was, when we were all ready to leave at the end of term, he told us that *we'd* have to pay for the repairs and he wouldn't give any of us our deposits back. He said that we'd caused the damage because of all the wild parties we'd been holding. And it was no use arguing because the neighbours had told him everything. But we hadn't had any parties, that was the point. We lived so far away from the uni that nobody wanted to come all the way out to our house for a party. So you'll never believe what we did. It was brilliant; Pete's idea. The morning we left we sprinkled grass seed all over the living room carpet. We used five packets, one each, and even moved the settee and chairs so that the stuff was absolutely everywhere. Then Pete watered it. I wish I could see the landlord's face when he goes to the house in September and realises he has to mow the living room.'

But she also talked a lot about proper things, adult things. She told me about the lecturers she admired the most at the university and about the different art exhibitions she'd been to. She talked a little bit about her work and the painting she was working on at the moment.

'It's all about nobody ever really being happy, how everybody always wants more than they've got. Nobody's satisfied any more. Especially when it comes to material things. It's all about that horrible 'keep up with the Joneses' attitude. And I blame the media; adverts on television and in magazines telling us we should always want more, that we can have anything we want. So I've cut pictures from magazines and painted around them. It's hard to explain, but I've tried to merge the two together within the picture and given it a kind of texture – our lecturer is always going on about textures. It's kind of anti-materialism. But you'll have to come round and see it, and give me your opinion.'

Nobody had ever talked to me about things like that before. With any other girl I'd be sitting waiting for a Jim Carrey film to start, not a Robert De Niro one. And the conversation would centre around the label and price tag on her new jumper, or she'd be telling me about how horrid her last boyfriend had been.

I watched Katie as she talked. She used her hands a lot to describe her stories, but it was her face that carried her words. It was so animated. Every expression started with those wonderful eyes of hers and seemed to ripple out across her cheeks, or down her nose to the tiny, jewelled stud, or up to her eyebrows and the soft lines of her brow. And every smile filled it completely. I was finding it difficult not to stare. But her eyes held me. Those almost unreal eyes, so large and blue. I couldn't believe she was with me, I was so lucky.

No, I told myself. It's not luck.

– What's not? –

I cringed, I kicked myself, I'd done it again. I tried to ignore him. The lights were beginning to slowly dim and the curtains drew back, opening up the screen for the first ten minutes or so of adverts. Katie excused herself and headed quickly for the toilet before the film started.

– Hey. Chris. You there or what? –

– No – I tried to concentrate on that terrible Bacardi ad they've been using for years. The appeal of the power was waning on me now. Paul was picking up a lot more than I wanted him to hear, and I didn't know how to stop it. I blamed our little experimentation and research; something had definitely happened there that had opened my mind up wider than before.

He laughed. – Look, I'm not hassling you, I promise –

– Yes, you are –

– No, come on, seriously, I'm not. I know you didn't want me to get in touch, it's just that I'm sat here with my fingers crossed and everything. I just wanted to know how things were going, that's all –

– Fine –

– Yeah? You reckon she likes you? That's great. I was just thinking though, you know, about how it'd be best to win her over? And I reckon . . . –

– You know what, Paul? I really wish you could see my face right now. I really wish I could send you the look on my face –

– Oh yeah? Why's that? –

148

– Because then you'd see how mad I am – I told him nastily.

– With me? – he asked.

– With you – I agreed.

– I was only trying to help –

– Well don't. I don't need your help –

– Oh, come on. Don't be like that –

– Like what? I'm not being like anything. You're the one with the problem –

– I just feel a bit left out – he told me. – That's all –

– Well, I'm sorry, Paul. But I guess that that's the way it is, okay? I just want this to be between me and Katie, no one else –

– But we've always done everything together –

– Maybe, but not this time. If this was a chapter in a book then it'd be Katie's chapter, okay? – I'd tried to make that last bit sound light-hearted, but I don't think it came across that way. – I just want it to be her – I sent. – Just me and her –

– But we're blood brothers. It's meant to be, you know, like in our song and everything –

– I didn't realise we had a song –

– Yeah, you do, I told you. That Bon Jovi one –

– And I told you, I can't stand Bon Jovi –

– But . . . –

– Just leave it, Paul. Okay? I really don't want to know –

I waited for him to answer back, but he'd gone again. I was angry, but I still felt a slight pang of regret that maybe I'd hurt him.

– Sorry – I sent.

It was true what he'd said; we had always done everything together. But somehow it had always been on his terms. I sat staring at the big screen, not taking in any of what was on it. Everything had always been Paul's idea, Paul's choice, Paul's game. In my eyes the partnership had never been exactly equal. It had never been Starsky and Hutch, more like Batman and Robin. And maybe I just wanted to be Batman for a change.

'You look tense.' Katie had reappeared next to me in the dark, I hadn't seen her coming. She slipped her hand into mine and leaned close to me across the seat's armrest. 'What's wrong?'

'Oh, nothing. I was just thinking.'

'Well stop it if it makes you frown. I've got a reputation to keep up, you know? I'm supposed to be a fun girl to be with.'

'You are,' I told her. 'The funnest I know.'

She grinned at this. 'It's been such a long time since I've done this,' she said. 'I haven't been on a date in absolutely ages.'

'I don't believe that,' I said with a smile. 'You must get asked out by lads all the time.'

She shook her head. 'Not any more.'

'I bet.'

'It's the truth. It's been . . .' She closed her eyes and calculated the length of time in her head. 'It's been at least six months since I've gone on a proper date. I'd forgotten how much fun they could be.'

'And this date's fun is it?' I asked.

'The funnest,' she told me.

I wanted to kiss her then. I wanted to *so* badly. And I think she wanted me to kiss her too. I think. But I didn't. Not yet, I decided, but later, after the film, don't push it. I gave her hand a quick squeeze instead. And she squeezed mine back. So I squeezed hers again. And again she squeezed mine, giggling. And this went on until the film started and the squeeze had become one long hand-hug.

I enjoyed the film, but I have to admit my mind was elsewhere and so the ending didn't quite add up for me. I was either a) watching Katie out of the corner of my eye, or b) expecting Paul to leap into my mind. Katie seemed to enjoy it. She thought the ending was great. She talked a lot, squeezed my hand a lot and generally made me feel on top of the world.

It was still warm when we left the cinema, and still quite light even though it was nearly ten o'clock. Katie hadn't let go of my hand yet. The longing to kiss her was so big it hurt. And I knew the right moment would come, I just wished it would hurry itself up a bit. There was no way I wanted the evening to end just yet and I suggested that we could maybe go for a drink or a pizza or something. Katie, however, had quite a different idea.

'Tollbar Roundabout?' I said, startled.

'Don't look at me like that,' she punched my arm gently. 'It's just . . .' She shrugged and offered me an embarrassed kind of laugh. 'It's just something I've always wanted to do. Ever since I was little. We used to drive past it every day on the way to school and I'd always think about it. And it is on the way home. If we walk the long way.'

'If that's what you really want to do,' I said, 'then who am I to argue?' It reminded me of something Paul would come up with. It was definitely the kind of bizarre idea he'd have.

'Haven't you ever thought about it yourself?' she asked. 'You must have driven by it hundreds of times.'

'It's not the kind of thing that usually crosses my mind,' I admitted.

'There's probably nothing there. I expect it's quite boring inside really.'

'Only one way to find out,' I told her, and we set off walking. Hand in hand. It'd only take us about twenty minutes to get there, but I was confident we could make it in about half an hour. If not longer.

She swung her arm backwards and forwards as we walked, taking mine with it, bringing our hands up quite high and making us almost march along. She was like an excited little schoolgirl. She chatted all the time, telling me more of her stories, asking me to tell her some juicy gossip about her brother, Matty. And I told her about the time he'd sneaked into the girls' changing room during Games. She couldn't stop laughing for ages, she gave herself a stitch and had to sit down on the kerb to ease it. But I'd missed out the part about Paul and me blackmailing him into it.

It got steadily darker, although not noticeably colder. The street lights pinged on one by one. We stood in the middle of Turner Road and watched them. And the twenty minute walk took us well over forty.

Tollbar Roundabout was basically just a big traffic island, but different. Most traffic islands are neatly kept, the council making sure the grass is bowling green smooth, the flowers pretty and bright, careful to remove ruts left by careless wheels. One year the island in the town centre even had 'CLEESTON TOWN' spelled out in daffodils around the edge (until some vandal had stamped on it and ripped up some of the letters so that it then read 'LEES TOWN' – but he was never caught and has forever remained fairly anonymous).

Tollbar Roundabout, however, was bigger than most and had large, unruly bushes around the edge. This could have been because the roundabout was on the outskirts of Cleeston and so the council couldn't be bothered with it, or maybe because the residents of the one or two houses that overlooked it simply preferred it that way. Whichever it was, it kept the island not exactly scruffy looking, but certainly unkempt, and as Katie and I approached it along Mayborough Road I understood exactly what she'd been talking about.

The bushes were tall and right on the edge of the roundabout, making a circle all the way around. They formed a kind of wall, and you could see that this perimeter of bushes were the only bushes on the island, there weren't any more on the inside of them. So what exactly was on the inside?

'I used to pretend there was a secret world in there,' Katie said. 'Like Narnia, except these were bushes you had to walk through and not a wardrobe. I used to beg my mum to stop the car and let me have a look, but she never would.'

There were very few cars moving around the island; this road out of Cleeston had never been a particularly busy one. We walked around it on the opposite side of the road, then stood on the pavement for a while just staring at the bushes. A couple of headlights flashed by us. We may have looked suspicious, maybe checking out the couple of houses on the far side of the road, but I for one certainly didn't care. My evening had been wonderful enough, and sitting next to Katie in the cinema I hadn't thought it could get much better. But this was something else. She was inviting me into her own private world. She was asking me to step with her into her childhood dreams and fantasies.

'What made you think of this place?' I asked her.

She shrugged. 'I don't know really. I suppose it was talking about old times and memories. This one simply jumped out at me. I haven't thought about it in such a long time. I suppose I drove past it so often that it gradually became less and less of something to think about.' She giggled. 'But I've certainly thought about it now. And there is no way I'm going to leave before I've been inside to see exactly what used to trouble me so much all those years ago.'

'It might be nothing.'

She kicked me in the shin. Not too softly either. 'Don't be such a spoilsport.' Then giggled again, tugging on my arm. 'Come on. I want you there to protect me from any nasty pixies or elves that could be lurking in there.' I wasn't about to refuse.

We waited for a car to go by, then trotted quickly across the road towards the traffic island. I felt like a kid again. There was that excited, nervous thrill running through my body, kind of like the feeling I got when Paul and I used to go garden creeping together when we were younger.

'We can get through here,' Katie said, holding back the tight branches, fighting through them. I followed her, having to scrap and scrabble all the way. And then we were standing inside.

It was maybe about as big as my bedroom, but circular. Maybe a bedroom in a lighthouse, I thought, with bushes for tall walls and a carpet of long grass. So it *was* empty inside, nothing really to see, but it still gave me the feeling of a secret world. A couple of cars drove around the roundabout; the beams of their headlights tried to pierce the cover of the bushes but were shattered and fragmented by the leaves and branches. They couldn't get through to us, not in here. No one could see us in here. I turned to look at Katie, to see her reaction. She was standing in the centre of the island, staring up into the night sky. I went over and stood next to her. I followed her gaze. The bushes were tall enough to block out most of the sky, we could only see what was directly above us. Not only did we have our own secret world, but it looked as though we had our own private patch of stars as well.

We sat down in the grass, still looking up at the night sky. Katie was smiling.

'It's . . .' she shrugged, looking for the right words. 'It's . . .'

'Kind of cool?' I offered.

And she nodded. 'Yes. I think it is.'

She was holding me with her eyes and I knew the right moment had come. So I leaned towards her and kissed her.

She didn't look shocked, she didn't act surprised. 'At last,' she whispered.

She put her arms around me, resting her head on my shoulder, then gently pulled me down into the grass with her. She was kissing my neck, my cheek and then my mouth. We lay so close together. I touched her hair, and it was as soft as I'd always imagined it to be. She unbuckled the front of her dungarees, pulled her T-shirt over her head. In the dim light her dark bra looked like a shadow falling across her pale skin. She kissed me again. Her hands held my face against hers. I touched her bra to make sure it was real, to prove to myself that it wasn't only a shadow after all, running my fingers down the strap from her shoulder.

'Don't tell me,' she said with a smile. 'I know it's too big for me. But I like to think of it as my "hopeful" bra.'

Everything seemed so right with her body, nothing clumsy, nothing obtrusive. It all seemed to fit so well. She unbuttoned the front of my shirt. My face felt hot. She had a little mole on her neck and I kissed it quickly, tentatively. Was I blushing? She ran her hands inside my shirt. I had plenty of moles on my chest, but she seemed determined to kiss every single one of them.

One car drove by, then a second, their headlights breaking around us, their engines dying away softly. The grass was cool, the stars very bright. She held me so close.

I was nervous. I'd never . . . I let Katie guide me. This is it, I thought to myself. This is it . . .

– Pop a wheelie! –

I felt as if I'd been kicked out of bed.

– Go for it, Chrissy-boy! –

I could have screamed. If Paul had been standing in front of me right there and then, I swear I would have probably ripped his head off.

'Chris? What's wrong?' Katie looked bewildered.

I shook my head. 'Nothing. Nothing's wrong.' But she could tell I was lying. The anger had made my body a statue next to hers, cold and rigid.

– Come on, what's happening? Tell us –

'I'm sorry, Katie.' I couldn't believe he was doing this to me. 'Maybe we should go. I'm so sorry.' I couldn't believe I was saying this. 'This doesn't mean . . .'

She stood up quickly. 'No, it's all right. I understand.'

– Come on, Chris. What's she look like? What's she doing? –

I stood up next to her. I went to touch her but the atmosphere between us had suddenly become tense, embarrassed. I had my head down, staring at my feet. I didn't watch as she climbed back into her T-shirt. She had it tucked into her dungarees before either of us would look at each other.

– Chris? –

I didn't know what to say to her. And she obviously didn't know what to say to me. We stood looking at each other in a dumb silence.

– Chris? You still there? –

Eventually I said, 'I've really had a good time tonight.' Because I had to say *something*. I shrugged. 'I've not felt like this in ages.' I gave her a quick grimace. 'I've *never* felt like this. I'd really like to see you again some time.'

157

She gave me a little, tight smile. Then stepped through the long grass towards the wall of hedges.

– Oh hell, have I . . .? Sorry, mate. I didn't mean . . . –

'I'll walk you home.'

She shook her head, tucking her hair behind her ear, but looking at the ground, not at me. 'No, it's okay. It's not too far from here.'

– I didn't realise . . . Look, I'm really . . . –

'Stay a while. Not long. Just . . . a few minutes.'

She shook her head again. 'I really should be getting home. I didn't realise how late it was.'

'I'll give you a ring.'

And at least she nodded this time. She waited for a car's head-lights to sweep by, and then was gone.

I slumped down into the grass with my head in my hands. I closed my eyes.

– Get out of my head – I told him. – Please, just get out of my head –

Chapter Fourteen

Bob Moody's not as big as his mate St. Pierre. Bob Moody's hair is dark and shaved very short, while St. Pierre's is a tight mass of greasy curls that look as though they'd chew up any comb that dared come within three feet of it. Bob Moody has big, brown eyes. St. Pierre has pieces of blue glass. Bob Moody somehow managed to pass his Technical Drawing GCSE. St. Pierre once ate my set-square and 2H pencil during TD. But believe it or not, when they're both kicking you it's actually quite difficult to tell them apart.

Why didn't I call for Paul? Because I didn't see them coming, I didn't have a chance.

They got me on the corner of Prince Street and Wright Street. It all happened so quickly, it was so unfair. I heard a yell from behind, I spun around, and St. Pierre punched me in the nose. My glasses exploded from my face. It hurt *so* much. I staggered backward, propelled more by the shock than by the actual force of the blow. I was literally seeing stars, green and red ones. He came at me again. I should have run then, taken to my heels and legged it for all I was worth. Maybe I should even have jumped over the garden wall next to me and knocked on whoever's door it was. But my mind went blank, the sense having been well and truly knocked out of me. I saw St. Pierre stepping forward and held up my hands to cover my face. So he punched me in the gut instead. And I crumpled up on myself, gasping for breath, only to have Bob Moody shoving me, shouting at me. He pushed me hard enough to knock me on to my backside. And that was when they both laid in with their feet.

Basically, I went down and stayed down. I didn't care how much yelling the pair of them did or how many different names they wanted to call me, there was no way I was going to stand up again. One of them stamped on my ankle while his mate kicked at my spine. I remember thinking: 'Okay guys, you've won, I'm on the floor, you've beaten me, you can stop kicking me now.' But that was about all I could think. The shock and the pain blazed away inside my head (the embarrassment would come later) leaving no room whatsoever for any other feelings or emotions. Even anger. Strangely enough I wasn't actually angry at Bob Moody and St. Pierre for what they were doing. I am now. Believe me, when I look back at the incident I still feel rage burning away inside of me. But at the time the only thing I could feel was surprised and hurt. And I guess when you think about it, it kind of makes sense. I mean, the gazelle who's brought down by the pack of hyenas won't feel particularly angry at his attackers. Just maybe a little disappointed that he was the one who got caught. And if he's going to feel angry at anyone shouldn't it really be at his mates? The other gazelles who legged it and left him to get caught?

After all, that's the way it was for me.

I reckon the two of them would quite easily have carried on kicking me all afternoon if it hadn't have been for some old bloke passing in his car.

'Hey, you lot! Hop it!' He'd pulled up on the opposite side of the road and was shouting from the safety of his red Vauxhall, but at least it stopped the kicking. 'Get out of here before I call the police!'

St. Pierre had turned to look across at him. Bob Moody was kneeling on me. He said: 'Tell your mate not to worry, we'll get him as well.' Then he stood up and had to physically drag St. Pierre away, who looked as though he was ready to start on the old bloke given half the chance.

I lay still with my cheek on the pavement and watched their big, heavy boots stomp away down the street. I wasn't sure whether I could move or not at first. I was still curled up and, very slowly, very tentatively, I tried to uncurl, starting with my legs. Every muscle told me not to. My whole body thought it was quite simply an act of madness to want to move. And the sun was pleasant and warm, so maybe I didn't need to move, maybe I could stay here, maybe have my meals brought to me where I lay? All I'd really need was a telly . . . But someone was shouting at me.

'Go on. We don't want your sort round here.' The man in his red Vauxhall was still there. 'I'll call the police.' I stared at him in disbelief.

He was waving his hand at me, shooing me away. 'Go on! Get out of here, you thug!' He didn't care if I was badly hurt or not, it wouldn't be his problem as long as I didn't die on the corner of his street.

So inch by agonizing inch I scraped myself off the pavement and somehow, with a lot of wincing and lip-biting, managed to get to my feet, unsteady as they were.

'Go on, I said,' the old man shouted. 'Get out of here.'

I picked my glasses up from out of the gutter (luckily they were still in one piece) and hobbled slowly, painfully, away. Taking my internal bleeding and cracked ribs and collapsed lung with me. Not that I turned out to have any of those things, but *he* didn't know that. He watched me shuffle all the way along Prince Street, then even followed me into Hampden Road and on to Duke Street in his shiny car just to make sure I left the estate. I guessed he was probably the head of the local Neighbourhood Watch Scheme. Or a bastard.

And it was all right for him to usher me out of his precious suburban street, but I didn't know whether or not Bob Moody and St. Pierre would be lurking around the next corner. I knew Bob Moody lived somewhere round here, I just didn't know where.

– Paul –

He didn't answer.

– Stop pratting about, I know you can hear me –

– Oh, hiya Chris. How're you? – We hadn't spoken since the incident at Tollbar Roundabout last night (he'd had the common decency, or the common sense, to leave me in peace) and he sounded a little hesitant.

– I need a lift –

– Oh, yeah, right. No problem. I'll be right there – He paused for a moment. – Er, were you trying to send to me a few minutes ago? –

– Not really, why? – I'd made my way to a bus shelter and sat myself down, taking the weight off my throbbing ankle.

– I just heard some really weird noises, that's all. I wondered if it was you –

– I'll tell you about it when you get here – I sent.

– Oh, okay. Where are you exactly anyway? – he asked.

– At a bus stop on Duke Street –

– What're you doing all the way over there? –

– I'll tell you when you get here –

– Okay, yeah – There was a pause, then he sent: – I've got something to tell you, too. You'll be dead chuffed –

'I doubt it,' I said out loud so he couldn't hear me.

– You see, I was thinking about what you were saying . . . –

– Tell me when you get here, will you? –

– Oh, yeah, right. Okay then. I won't be long –

While I was waiting for Paul I spent the time either keeping an eye out in case Bob Moody and St. Pierre reappeared or prodding myself to see exactly where and how much I hurt. My nose wasn't bleeding and didn't feel broken, although it was so sore I reckoned it should have been. My ankle was painful too, but it looked as though my biggest bruises would be on my back where St. Pierre had been putting his boot in. And even though my whole body felt as if it'd been run over, I guessed I'd been pretty lucky really. But it didn't stop the anger from growing bigger and bigger and focusing itself even more acutely on Paul. I knew I wouldn't be sitting in a bus shelter on Duke Street with size eleven boot prints running up and down my spine if it wasn't for Paul.

If he hadn't have been pratting about with Jane Lois-Lane at Matty Harker's party then Bob Moody wouldn't have chased him around the comp the other day, and I wouldn't have had to go to his rescue, clobbering St. Pierre to help him escape. And I wouldn't even be in this part of town if he hadn't ballsed it up for me last night with Katie. I'd been on my way to her house to apologise when I was jumped. And I only went to his rescue because of the power. And he only managed to balls it up for me because of the power. The power that he'd forced me to have when we'd become blood brothers.

It took Paul a little over fifteen minutes to reach me. Fifteen minutes in which my anger mushroomed. How come he was able to catch loose thoughts last night when I'd been with Katie, and yet all he claimed he'd heard today was 'weird noises'? Had he done it on purpose? The more I thought about it, the more he was to blame. By the time he pulled up in front of the bus shelter I was seething.

– Hey, hey, hey. How're you doing? – he greeted me cheerfully. But his smile soon disappeared when he saw the way I hobbled over to the car and he became suddenly very anxious. – What's happened to you? – he asked. – You've got black eyes –

I climbed into the passenger seat and snapped down the sun visor. The little mirror embedded into the black PVC admitted he was telling the truth. I had big, dark, painful looking (and feeling) bruises underneath my eyes from where my nose had been slammed so hard by St. Pierre's fist.

'I was going to see Katie,' I told him as he pulled away from the curb. It was a chore to contain my anger, but I was determined to tell him the full story. 'I thought I'd better apologise to her for what happened last night and . . .'

– Did I mess it up bad? Look I'm really sorry, I really didn't mean to – He glanced over at me, trying to gauge the expression on my face. – But I'm sure you'll sort it out with her, she seems nice enough. But I really am dead sorry. You know me, sometimes I can be just so – and he made a dumb noise to try and explain just how dumb he thought he could be. Personally though, I reckoned he should have made it sound a hell of a lot dumber than he did.

'Yeah, well I didn't actually make it all the way to her house, you see. Mainly because . . .'

– I'm sure she'll understand – he sent, nodding his head. He took a left on Cromwell Avenue. – She probably wouldn't want to see you looking like that anyway –

I was confused. 'Is that meant to reassure me?'

He looked at me nonplussed. – Eh? –

I shook my head. 'Don't worry about it,' I said nastily. 'But as I was saying . . .'

– You're still angry at me, aren't you? –

I nearly laughed. 'You could say that.'

– But not for long. 'Cos I've got some news that's gonna cheer you up for definite –

'Look, Paul, I . . .'

– No, no, shut up. You'll be . . . –

'Paul, if you're . . .'

– I've asked Jane Lois-Lane out – he sent. He actually looked quite pleased with himself. – I phoned her up this morning and asked her, because of what you said – He pulled up at the traffic lights on Clark Street and was waiting for some kind of a reaction from me, but I didn't have one at the time. – You know, you've been saying that I ought to stop messing around and meet someone properly, get to know them, like you're trying to do with Matty's sister. So now me and Jane are kind of an item – He was grinning at me from the driver's seat of his father's Sierra. – It's weird, but I've never had a proper girlfriend before. And Jane's all right, she's dead pretty and that. And if I'm going out with her then we don't have to worry about Bob Moody or anything 'cos she'll dump him straight away. Smart move, don't you think? –

I could have hit him. I really, honestly could. 'Paul, it was Bob Moody who . . .'

– But you know what the best thing'll be? – he sent as the lights changed and he shot away down the road. – We can still get to go out together, instead of it being like it was last night. We can go out as a foursome. You and me, Jane and Katie. And I was thinking that maybe tonight we could go bowling, because we haven't been in ages, have we? I reckon it'll be a good night – He started laughing. – That's if Katie doesn't mind being seen in public with you looking like that –

I blew up. I hit the roof. I went ballistic. I don't think Paul knew what hit him. It all kind of burst out of me. He just sat there, driving me home, his face quite pale, silent. And he took it all, every little scrap of abuse I had to give him.

Chapter Fifteen

Monday morning. So much was going to happen before Tuesday.

Just before I woke I'd been dreaming. I wasn't sure about what exactly, but there was a peculiar feeling that it had been important and I needed to remember it. Had it been about the headache? Or had the headache woken me up? But now that I was awake the headache had disappeared, leaving me with the kind of lull or peaceful sensation you get after a thunderstorm. I ducked my head under the duvet to escape from the sunlight creeping around the edges of the curtains, but it was like trying to hold ice cubes in a warm hand and the dream soon melted away.

I peeped out from my huddle of bed clothes at the clock on my wall. 9:48. I didn't feel like there was anything worth getting up for just yet and let myself drift off to sleep again. Maybe to dream a little more.

I woke again a little over an hour later, just before eleven. The phone was ringing, my hand was throbbing, I wasn't sure which one had roused me from my sleep. The phone was answered downstairs which then left me with silence and the hurt in my hand. The ache it gave me reminded me all too well of the rest of my body's complaints and I got up slowly to check my bruises and wounds in the mirror on the back of my wardrobe door. They'd settled overnight into a deep, ugly purple. My eyes cast nasty black shadows. I ached all over. It was as though I'd slept on a concrete bed, with lumps in it. I saw every mark on my body as yet another black mark against Paul. And believe me, I had a lot of marks on my body. But it was the throbbing in my hand that worried me the most, I knew all too well what it could signify. I wasn't bleeding though, the scab on my palm was still clean, still unbroken, but the hurt was deep. So what was Paul up to? Was he trying to get inside my head without me knowing?

– You'd better not be! – I sent him nastily.

I didn't bother opening my curtains. I was in no mood for glorious sunshine today. Just like I was in no mood to have Paul messing around with my mind.

– I mean it! Don't you dare –

Although my explosion of anger had been sudden and although what I'd said had been incredibly brash, I'd spent most of last night telling myself that I'd meant every word. He'd pushed me too hard, too far, once too often. I'd made a decision. I'd told him I wished I'd shared my blood with Katie instead. If I'd maybe thought my words through properly I would have told him that I wanted to be with Katie

169

more than I wanted to be with him, but it all boiled down to the same thing. I was eighteen, my father had married when he'd been only two years older – my mother only four years older when she'd given birth to Robert. I wasn't at school anymore, I was going away to university and leaving him here in Cleeston. It was about time I grew up. I'd told him all of this. He'd been like a stray dog that you can't get rid of. You stroke it just the once and then can't stop it from following you, no matter how many times you shoo it away. The only way to make it go is to hurt it.

There was a slice of sunlight across my carpet. It came from the crack of curtains at the centre of the pelmet. I could see dust particles dancing in the brightness. I used to believe they were fairies when I was a kid. It was scary to think how gullible you could be.

A small knock at my door shook me from my thoughts. My mother asked if I was decent but didn't wait for a reply before she came in. I was expecting a lecture about being up so late, but didn't get one. She opened my curtains, straightened the bed clothes, picked up yesterday's socks off the floor from the foot of my bed and put them in the wash basket before she even spoke to me.

She saw me cradling my hand. 'Is it still troubling you?' she asked.

I nodded. 'I must've slept on it funny.'

But this obviously wasn't a good enough explanation for my mother. She came over to inspect it. 'I can't understand why it hasn't healed yet,' she told me. She poked at the cut. 'You might have to let Dr Wheeler look at it after all. Is it very painful?'

'It'll be okay.' I tried unsuccessfully to pull it away from her.

'But it's started weeping,' she said. And when I looked at it again I realised my palm was damp and sticky with a strange, watery fluid. 'Come on, I'll put a bandage on it for you.' She took me through into the bathroom and I sat on the edge of the bath in silence while she dressed my hand. 'If it doesn't get any better soon I'm taking you to the doctor's myself,' she told me finally.

I was about to get up and go back through into my bedroom when she said, 'How are the rest of your war wounds? Let me have a look.'

I sighed and let her poke me about a bit more, inspecting the bruises on my back.

'I don't understand why you won't let your father talk to their parents about this,' she tutted. 'Look at the mess they've made of you. God help them if I ever get my hands on them.'

'Can I go now?'

She stopped prodding at my spine and stood up straight. She started rolling up the excess bandage so she could fit it back into its little box again. 'That was Paul's mother on the phone.'

I looked at her suspiciously. Had Paul said something about our argument? Was this going to be some sort of kiss and make up speech on his behalf? Because if it was, then . . .

'He's been in an accident. She was phoning from the hospital.' She sat down next to me on the edge of the bath. 'I think he's in a pretty bad way.'

Of course I felt bad, it's ludicrous to think I'd feel anything else but bad. This was Paul we were talking about. And yet . . .

My mother was sitting close to me but I wouldn't look at her. I looked at the blue and white tiles on the bathroom floor instead.

'He's been knocked off his bike. I'm not sure where it happened, Lynne didn't say. She was beside herself. He was on his way to meet some girl or other earlier this morning, about quarter to ten I think. Do you know who that could have been?' I shook my head automatically, then suddenly realised it was probably Jane Lois-Lane, but didn't say anything. I stared at the tiles. I did feel bad, I told myself, I really did. But . . .

'The traffic in this town is getting worse and worse,' my mother was saying. 'Your father's forever complaining about it.' She shook her head and let out a long sigh, her breath trembling. 'Lynne was beside herself. And I thought about you coming home yesterday all battered and bruised and the way I'd felt when I'd seen you . . . The poor woman must be going through hell.' She was dabbing at her eyes with her curled first finger. She wasn't crying at the moment, but the horrible prospect of it hung over me in the bathroom, misting up the mirrors, and I simply had to get up and leave. Not because my mother's tears might embarrass me, but because the lack of any from me certainly would.

I went back into my bedroom and sat at my desk staring out of my window at the street and the houses opposite. I picked up a pencil and rolled it around between my fingers. I tapped it against the desk top. Of course I felt bad. It went without saying. I wouldn't have wished for this. Never. Not in a million years. So it was obvious I felt bad. But . . .

But I also felt so very, very numb.

My mother knocked quietly at my bedroom door. I expected her to come straight in just as she always did, but she knocked again.

'Come in.'

She opened the door but didn't step inside the room. 'I promised Lynne we'd go to the hospital this afternoon, just to see if there's anything we can do to help.'

I had my back to her. 'Yeah. Thanks.'

She hesitated at the door a moment longer. Everybody knew how close Paul and I had been, our parents more than most thanks to the trouble we'd often got ourselves into together (and the lengths we'd gone to get each other out of it). So I was expected to take this news especially hard.

She took a small step towards me. 'Can I get you a drink or something? You haven't had your breakfast yet.'

I shook my head, still not turning round to face her.

'Well, if there's anything . . .' But she forced herself to let me deal with my feelings on my own and closed the door behind her.

I scribbled on the desk top with the pencil, then licked my finger and quickly rubbed the mark away. I looked up as a car drove past outside. Was that the one which had knocked Paul from his bike? It turned left at the top of the street onto the crescent, heading in the direction of the school.

I felt strangely detatched. I felt as if I'd stepped off the world and let it turn a couple seconds in time ahead of me before I'd climbed back on board. I wasn't experiencing real emotions, they'd burned and

173

died before I'd reached them. I was only haunted by their fragile ghosts as the ever-turning world carried me through where they'd been.

Shouldn't I be crying? Wasn't I supposed to already be on my way to the hospital to see Paul, to find out exactly how badly hurt he was? Shouldn't there be some sort of pain for me?

The lack of tears, the lack of feeling, I told myself it could only mean one thing. It could only mean that the friendship was over between us. He really had pushed me too far. My anger at him was by far stronger than my concern for him. The chapter in my life that had been Paul was closing rapidly. It was the only explanation.

I was scribbling with my pencil, jagged little lines, then rubbing them away. My fingertip was a mucky grey. I'd been putting this off since my mother had told me what had happened. But now I closed my eyes and sent to him.

– Paul? –

– –

There was nothing; no static, no white noise, not even the sound of his breathing which would sometimes come through to me.

– Paul? –

– –

– Can you hear me? –

– –

Was he sleeping? Could he be ignoring me because of yesterday's little fracas? Or had the accident been bad enough to make him lose the power?

I poked at my bandaged hand with the point of the pencil. The cloth was damp with the sticky, viscous fluid the wound was weeping. I pushed the point underneath the bandages, poking at the wound Paul had inflicted on me, hurting myself on purpose. The pain was acute, increasing the throbbing sensation, sharpening the ache. I wondered if I could make myself bleed out his blood and lose the power. The idea was disturbing, but not enough to make me cry. And I was certain that that was what I was supposed to be doing. My best friend in a road accident, in hospital. My blood brother.

Had I seen this coming? Had I known it was going to happen? Maybe not, but I told myself that ever since meeting Katie I may have wanted it to.

And right now it was Katie who I wanted to be with. She would be the final proof that I was right, that what was happening was inevitable, was simply growing up. I wanted her to make me feel the way she had on Saturday night. I'd been all right for emotion then; stuffed with it, brimming over. I wouldn't be numb with her by my side.

Chapter Sixteen

This time I kept my eyes open, and went by a different route. I had an inkling that Bob Moody lived pretty close to where he and St. Pierre had cornered me yesterday so stayed on the bus that extra stop or two and went the long way round, cutting across the back of the old people's home on Alderleigh Way.

I'd slipped out of the house without telling my mum; I really didn't think I'd be able to explain to her exactly what was going on inside my head. It meant I'd be in trouble with her when I got home, but I reckoned everything would be so much clearer and easier to explain after I'd seen Katie. Maybe I'd even take her home with me, invite her for tea, I was sure my parents would like her.

She lived on Lichfield Road. I'd actually been to her house a couple of times; once because of the party, but once before that too, in Year Nine. Paul and I had gone back after school one day to see Matty's new Scalextric, but Paul had accidentally stood on one of the cars (it was a Jaguar with working lights and sound effects) snapping it in two and we'd never been invited back. It was weird to think that neither of us had ever known Matty had a sister. It made me wish I'd become proper friends with him instead of just classmates, because then maybe I would have met her a long time before now. I was wondering whether I'd be able to change my choice of university, go to Manchester with Katie instead.

I was trying not to think too much about Paul. There was part of me that still didn't trust him. To tell the truth I wouldn't have put it past him to have made the whole story up about being knocked off his bike and taken to hospital, just to make me feel sorry for him. I still wasn't wholly sure he wouldn't leap into my mind at any given moment and shriek some kind of obscenity. Just to wind me up. I was trying to file him away, put him deep down at the back of my mind, like I'd done with so many other things recently. It wasn't really working, but I kept on trying.

I walked slowly down Lichfield Road. Katie's house was about three quarters of the way along; big, white and detatched. I wondered briefly if maybe I should have phoned to let her know I was coming, but then she *had* invited me round to see her new painting. Well, sort of, anyway. There was a new Escort parked out front, metallic blue, all the trimmings. I guessed her father must have been splashing out a bit recently. His old car, an especially boxy Lada, had been the bane of Matty's life at school.

I was nervous as I closed the small, wooden gate behind me and headed up the drive. I'd always hated calling for girls; it was their fathers who scared me. I'd never known one yet who'd looked kindly on me as a gentleman caller for his daughter. It was the way they stared at me, their eyes travelling up and down, everything from polish of shoes to parting of hair scrutinised, trying to assess background, prospects and motives. I'd learned a few years ago that 'I'll meet you there' was so much easier than 'I'll pick you up'. So when I knocked a little bit tentatively on the front door I was sincerely hoping Mr Harker was at work and nowhere within earshot. And then while I was standing waiting I suddenly realised that the last time I'd seen this doorstep it had been under rather more peculiar circumstances. So you can understand why I visibly sighed when Matty answered the door.

'Hiya, Chris.' He looked surprised that it was me knocking on his door. 'Haven't seen you in a while.'

'No,' I said. 'I've been a bit busy.'

He nodded, his lank fringe falling into his eyes. 'Yeah, me too. My dad's forced me to get a job at this pub in town. It's okay, like. But it's still work, you know what I mean? You'll have to come in and see me some time.'

'Yeah,' I said. 'I will.' I realised that I probably would see a bit more of Matty anyway, now that Katie and I were so close. And I felt bad for picking on him when we'd been younger. He was a good kid. Although to be honest, the taunts had always been Paul's idea.

'Er, listen, Matty. I actually came to see Katie. Is she in?'

'No, she's not.' He saw my face fall. 'But she should be back any minute, like. You can wait if you want,' he said. 'Craig's waiting for her anyway.'

'Craig?' I asked suspiciously.

'Yeah. He's at her uni. He's all right, like. You'll get on well with him.' He ushered me in through the front door.

I recognised 'Craig' straight away, although he wasn't wearing his tartan shirt today (it was an equally horrid watery purple instead). He was sitting in the over-soft settee Paul and I had spent most of our time slouched in at the party, and nodded at me as I followed Matty into the living room. The early showing of *Neighbours* was on the telly and he turned back to it.

'Craig Johnson, this is Chris Ganin. Chris, this is Craig,' Matty said, ever friendly.

I offered a 'Now then, mate,' but Johnson didn't offer anything more than the short nod he'd already felt obliged to give me; his eyes were on the TV. I sat next to him and the settee dragged me down in to its cushioned clutches.

Matty sat himself down in the armchair opposite. 'So, what've you been doing with yourself, like?' he asked before noticing the black marks half hidden by my glasses and the bandage wrapping my right hand. Then it was: 'Hey, you been in a fight or what?'

'Yeah,' I said. 'Something like that.'

Johnson gave me a cursory glance, snorted a small, derisive chuff through his fat nose and turned back to *Neighbours*. He was a tall kid, much taller than me. I tried to somehow equal his height by sitting up straighter than him, but the marshmallow of a settee simply wouldn't allow it. His dark hair was groomed to perfection, he'd never seen a zit in his life and you could have balanced your pint on his jaw. He was the type of kid Paul and I had always loathed.

'So, how'd it happen?' Matty asked.

I wanted to tell Matty the truth, about Bob Moody and Paul and Jane Lois-Lane, but I really didn't want to admit anything in front of whoever the hell this Johnson kid thought he was. I didn't think he recognised me from Swift's, but I found myself wishing he did. I wanted him to remember that Katie had been dancing with me, not him. Or at least had been until Paul had messed it up for me. And this thought only gave me a couple more bricks to help build the wall in my head that was keeping my ex-best friend out of my mind.

'Did you have a good night up Swift's on Saturday?' I asked the guy sitting next to me, ignoring Matty's question.

He gave me a long look then, trying to place my face. 'Were you there as well?' he asked in an accent I didn't recognise, but which was probably southern.

I nodded. 'That's right. I was with Katie.'

He chuffed at me through his nose again. 'Oh. Yeah. I remember.' He turned back to the screen.

'When did it happen?' Matty asked.

'Yesterday,' I said without looking at him – I was also staring at the telly. 'So what brings you to Cleeston, Craig?' I asked, pretending I didn't already know, making out as if I hadn't already sussed his slimey intentions.

'Katie,' he said slowly, letting a small grin slide its way across his face. He folded his arms and rested back into the spongy grip of the settee.

I knew it. I could have laughed. Here he was, all the way from the Home Counties and acting like the old university chum, trying to insinuate his way into Katie's favour. Smooth-talking, easy listening, a hint of sensitivity and rent-a-hunk good-looks. I was sitting next to the competition, so I had to play it cool. But I was confident too, after what had happened between Katie and me on Saturday night. I doubted if Mr Johnson here had ever even heard of Tollbar Roundabout. I wasn't going to let him steal Katie away from me. I'd beaten him on the dance floor at Swift's and I could beat him in the Harkers' living room. After all, this was the place I'd first seen Katie, I'd been sitting on exactly the same settee, so this was kind of home turf for me.

I think Matty could feel the tension growing in the air. 'Er, yeah,' he said, fidgeting in the armchair, continually sweeping his greasy fringe higher on to his forehead. 'Yeah, Craig's been staying for a couple of days, like. Goes home tomorrow though, don't you?'

Johnson shrugged. 'I'm not sure yet,' he said in that accent of his. 'Katie mentioned that I might be able to stay on a little while longer, if your parents agreed.'

I hoped he choked on that plum in his mouth. 'You're on Katie's course at university, are you?' I asked.

'We're both Fine Art,' he told me, without looking at me. 'But I'm more sculpture based, while Katie prefers painting. She's quite the little Van Gogh.' He pronounced the name 'Van Go'.

'I bet she is,' I said. I saw Matty about to open his mouth but jumped in before him. 'She's told me all about her latest painting. That's why I'm here actually. She invited me round to see it. She wanted me to tell her what I thought of it.'

Johnson deigned to look at me. 'You've had a lot experience with art then, have you?'

'No,' I admitted. 'I think she just values my opinion.'

Again the derisory snort through his nose. I was feeling tense. There was a flicker of anger inside me. I couldn't believe the arrogance of this kid, stumped-up sap that he was. I wasn't going to let him steal Katie away. No way. No how.

Matty had managed to fidget himself to his feet. 'Hey, er, does anyone want a drink, like? I'll put the kettle on, you know?' But the two of us on the settee shook our heads and he stood awkwardly for a moment not knowing exactly what to do. Then his face lit up when he came up with another good reason to leave the room. 'I'll tell you what, why don't I go get Katie's painting?' He was moving for the door already. 'You'll like it, Chris, it's dead good.'

'I really don't think you should be exhibiting Katie's work when she isn't here,' Johnson said.

But Matty was already in the hall. 'Nar, she won't mind. She shows her pictures to everybody.'

Which left me alone with Johnson. I was staring at the television, but I wasn't seeing anything; Ramsey Street was just a noise in the background. Now was my chance to lean across, grab him by the collar and tell him to get the hell out. But I didn't think violence was going to be necessary. Saturday night had been kind of magical, I was sure

Katie had felt it too. And I'd helped to provide that feeling. I doubted Johnson could reproduce it. That evening had been my first taste of something very special, and I'd given up my friend to be able to taste it again. I wasn't going to let this guy move in on Katie with his swanky charm and Oscar-nominated face. When I'd been lying at her feet in the bathroom, even with alcohol churning my insides, I'd known I could fall in love with her. And that was exactly what I aimed to do.

We sat in silence. Johnson didn't seem in the least bit concerned by my presence and I decided that his over-confidence was going to be his downfall. Not every woman was won over by money and swagger. Especially not one like Katie. I couldn't wait for Matty to appear with her anti-materialism painting.

And with that thought I suddenly realised whose metallic blue Escort it was parked in the road. I felt quite smugged-up and brimming over when I asked: 'Is that your car out front?'

Johnson nodded. 'Yes.' He glanced out of the window at it as it rested in the gutter. He was probably worried I'd scratched it on my way in. I wished I had. I'd do it on the way out, I told myself. With Katie holding my hand.

'Nice,' I said.

'Thank you.'

I smiled at him. 'Katie like it, does she?'

'Yes, she does.' He returned my smile. 'In fact, she chose it for me. I was after something a little smaller myself, a little Peugeot I'd got my eye on. But Katie talked me into the Escort, and I'm quite satisfied with it so far.' He winked at me. 'More leg room, if you see what I mean.'

I could have smacked him. How dare he make suggestive remarks about Katie? He wasn't fit to wipe the dirt from her cherry-reds. And I was ready to tell him so too, but Matty appeared just in time.

'This is it,' he said and rested the painting on the arms of the armchair, propping it up against the back. 'What d'you reckon?' he asked me.

I leaned forward in my seat to look.

It was painted on an off-white canvas and stretched across a wooden frame. It was about three feet long and two feet high. It was a swirl of colour, the brush strokes visible. I could see the magazine cuttings Katie had talked about, layered up over one other, some obscuring the other's image; half a sunbed poking out from behind a picture of a microwave, wrinkled and torn at the edges. It looked hectic. The paint splashed across the photographs from the magazines. The colours merged, building on top of each other, the strokes looking nasty, heavy-handed. It all looked like a bit of a mess to me.

'And what opinion will you be passing on to Katie?' Johnson asked.

I paused, as if in consideration. 'I really like the use of texture,' I said.

I wasn't at all sure what Johnson made of my statement, but Matty seemed impressed. 'Wow, yeah,' he said. 'I hadn't thought of that.' He ran his fingers lightly over the thick painted scrawls. 'And what d'you reckon it's about, like? What's it mean?'

I shrugged, but in a considered way, still leaning forward, my elbows on my knees and my hands clasped. I almost said 'anti-materialism' but I was cleverer than that. 'It looks as though she had a bit of an anti-consumerism bee in her bonnet at the time,' I said. Then sat back in the settee.

'Ha! Well, you're wrong there,' Matty said. 'It's actually against materialism and stuff.' He pushed that irritating fringe of his from out of his eyes again. 'I think. But don't worry, like. Because I didn't get it until she told me either.'

Johnson looked at me, ignoring Matty. 'Katie *will* be pleased,' he said. I got the feeling I hadn't fooled him for a second.

I told myself not to get angry. I told myself to relax, not to worry, to think about Tollbar Roundabout and about how much it had meant. But I had the strange sensation that there was something I didn't quite grasp about this situation, something greasy and evasive that kept slipping through my fingers.

'Good though, isn't it?' Matty said putting the painting on the floor and sitting in the armchair.

'Yes, it's very good,' I lied.

Matty seemed to feel as though he'd eased the tension now. He seemed quite pleased with himself. 'Hey, if you like it that much, Chris, why don't you ask Katie if she'll let you have it?'

I didn't get a chance to speak, Johnson jumped in ahead of me. 'I'm afraid it's already spoken for,' he said.

'Oh, right. You having it, like?' Matty asked.

Johnson merely nodded.

I shrugged. I was desperate to get one up on him, determined to knock that condescending glaze from out of his eyes. 'You never know,' I said. 'Maybe she'd like me to have it.'

'No offence,' Johnson assured me. 'But I'm afraid we've already picked the exact spot to hang it.'

'Oh yeah?' Matty put in pleasantly. 'Where's that?'

And without warning the conversation took two sudden, rapier-like strokes at my heart.

'Katie wants it in our bedroom,' Johnson said. 'Above the chest of drawers.'

'I bought that chest of drawers for them,' Matty told me. 'When they first moved in together. It'd look good there.'

'Oh,' I said.

I sat quite still, and I certainly didn't know what else to say. My 'oh' hung in the air, echoing within its own absurdity. There was something akin to butterflies in my stomach, but their wings were so very sharp. I thought I heard a dull thud inside my head as a final piece fell heavily into place.

And if the last exchange had involved graceful cuts with a sword at my heart, the words that followed were simply bombs planted underneath my ego.

'So how long's it you've been living together now?'

'Six months.'

I was crumbling away inside. I could feel myself folding up right there on the over-soft settee, and I wished it would suck me away into oblivion. Katie had told me she hadn't been on a proper date in about six months, so I guess it hadn't *technically* been a lie.

'And you're still planning on getting engaged, like?'

'On her twenty-first birthday, yes.'

'Wow, I've never been a brother-in-law before.'

I closed my eyes. They talked on about things I really didn't want to listen to.

Even through the hurt I realised it would be easy for me to tell Johnson about what had happened between Katie and me, about how willing she had been to give herself to me. It could split them up. It would certainly cause problems for them. And part of me, some prickly spiteful part of me hiding low inside, wanted this. But it would have taken anger to raise those particular words and my anger had been the first thing to crumble away. Maybe I'd used it all up. Maybe I'd simply run out of anger, it had all drained away. Because when you thought about it, it certainly seemed to have been all I'd felt for the past couple of days.

I tried to dredge some up from somewhere, I really did. But the thought of Katie was crushing me. I realised that it wasn't Johnson who'd been trying to steal Katie away from me, but the other way around. I'd been the bad guy in this situation. But only because of Katie's lies.

I surprised myself with my passivity. And in fact it was kind of a relief not to have to be angry any more. But God, how it hurt. The world around me was heavy and thick and claustrophobic.

So I decided to keep as much dignity as I could. I told myself that

I would keep the night with Katie inside our private world of Tollbar Roundabout all to myself. A reminder of how special I could feel. She may have used me, but at least she'd given me something in return.

'And remember the first time you came to stay?' Matty was saying. He was full of good memories.

Johnson smiled and nodded. 'Your parents' first impression of me wasn't exactly a wonderful one, was it?' I knew he was only reminiscing for my benefit.

'I tell you, Chris. You won't believe what happened,' Matty said. 'I thought my dad was going to explode, like.'

'What happened?' I forced myself to ask, trying to make believe the conversation wasn't really pulling apart my insides.

Johnson moved to explain, but Matty was too full of the story to let anybody else tell it. 'Dad wouldn't let them sleep together,' he told me. ' "Not in this house", you know what I mean? So they sneaked out, didn't you Craig?' He didn't wait for a reply. 'Got themselves a sleeping bag and sneaked off to Tollbar Roundabout, like. Didn't you? You know the one I mean? Out on Mayborough Road? It's empty inside, you see. Me and Katie used to play in it when we were younger. But a copper spotted them sneaking in and . . .'

I didn't hear any more of the story. I stood up. I was suddenly scared I was going to cry.

'Listen, Matty.' The words stuck. I had to clear my throat. 'I really should get going. I've, you know . . .' I held my breath, capturing a sob and not letting it free. 'Just say hi to your sister from me, okay?'

'She'll be back any minute. She'll want to see you.'

I shrugged. I doubted it. 'Sorry,' I said weakly. I walked unsteadily out into the hall. I didn't say goodbye to Johnson. I couldn't bear to look at him.

And then just before I reached the front door, Matty following me down the hallway, it opened. And Katie stepped in.

We stared at each other. She looked blurred to me, it was the water in my eyes. But still beautiful. Her cheeks were ruddy, caught by the sun, her eyes wide, blue, child-like. Still so very, very beautiful. I was fighting with my breath as it hitched in my throat.

She tucked her hair behind her ear as was her custom.

'Chris came to see your painting,' Matty chirped from over my shoulder. 'I showed it to him. I hope you don't mind, like.'

Katie shook her head. 'Not at all,' she said. She could see the tears welling in my eyes. She didn't need to be a genius to guess what must have happened. 'What did you think?'

I needed to blink, but knew that if I did the tears would brim over and run down my cheeks. I was trembling slightly. And from somewhere deep, deep inside I found an ounce of defiance.

'I think it's shit,' I told her truthfully, and stepped outside.

– Paul? –

– –

– Paul, please, if you can hear me . . . –

– –

– Oh God, Paul. If you can hear me please say. Please, Paul. I'm so sorry. I thought I could . . . I really need to talk to you, Paul –

‑ ‑

‑ Please, I'm begging you, say if you can hear me ‑

‑ ‑

‑ I need you, Paul. I need you so bad right now ‑

‑ ‑

‑ I'm so sorry . . . ‑

PART FIVE

Chapter Seventeen

I guess what happened next is the kind of stuff legends are made of. And I know that the many times afterward whenever Paul and I have related the story we have always managed to augment even the tiniest of details. Paul's depictions of the action have always been more flamboyant than mine, of course. But then again, he was the hero of the piece.

The barn was hot, dark and smelly. The farmer had been gone for at least half an hour, and my mind was turning tricks on me, imagining all kinds of punishments I could suffer at the hands of both parents and police alike. The queasiness in my stomach hadn't subsided, in fact the more I thought about the trouble I was in the worse it got. My dad's favourite punishment had always been grounding me, but I knew this was going to be much, much worse than having to stay in my bedroom for a couple of days . . .

Suddenly the locked door was rattled from the outside.

I stayed very still, waiting for it to be flung open, waiting for the farmer or a policeman or both to burst in. But the small wooden door wasn't opened. I stayed quiet. Then it was rattled again.

I got to my feet slowly and edged my way over to the door. There was a knothole in the wood where a beam of sunlight fell through and I put my eye to it. I could see out on to the large yard, the back of the farmhouse and the back end of the tractor with the trailer of hay. But there was nobody there.

'Paul?' I whispered. Then a little bit louder. 'Paul? Is that you?'

There was no answer. But I could hear somebody moving around out there. I could hear footsteps skirting around the side of the barn. I squirmed against the knothole, wanting to see a wider view than it would give me, switching from my right to my left eye and back again, trying to follow the sound of the footsteps.

'Paul. Hey, Paul. Is that you?'

'Don't worry. Just get ready to run.'

'What's happening. What's going on?'

'Quick, shush. He's coming back.'

Through my spy-hole I saw the back door of the farmhouse open and the farmer emerge. He'd changed out of his smelly overalls and rubber galoshes into a pair of normal jeans and work boots, but the expression on his face was still the same; he still looked as mad as hell. He stalked his way across the yard towards the barn. I ducked back away from the door just in time before the farmer flung it wide.

'I'd look worried too, if I were you, laddy,' he said. But it wasn't actually him I was looking at.

I saw Paul step into view behind the farmer. He was a silhouette in the bright sunlight as it fell through the barn door. He was carrying something small but awkward in his hands. The farmer noticed me looking over his shoulder. He turned round to see what I was staring at. And at exactly the same moment Paul heaved the water-bomb at him.

I suddenly realised where he'd been for the last half an hour or so. He'd been back at my house preparing it, raiding my mother's cupboards for ingredients (I could only hope she hadn't seen what he was up to). He was a bit of a master when it came to water-bombs; his weren't just balloons filled with water, but true weapons. This particular one had first been half-filled with talcum powder, toothpaste and anti-dandruff shampoo before being topped up with Uncle Ben's Sweet and Sour Sauce. Putting water in water-bombs had always been much too simple for Paul.

The balloon had been yellow, but it's contents had turned it a rather darker, orangey colour. And it had been aimed at the farmer's back, between his shoulder blades. The problem was he'd seen it coming, tried to duck out of its way, and so got it full in the face. He howled as it burst its muck across his brow.

'RUN!' Paul shrieked.

The farmer made a fumbled grab at me, the mess getting in his eyes. I dodged him easily. Paul grabbed my arm and hauled me out into the yard. The farmer was bellowing his rage behind us. He'd already proved he wasn't a man to give up easily, we knew we had a chase on our hands.

'Go, go, go!' Paul was shouting. 'He's coming.'

We ran across the yard back towards the fields, but the farmer didn't follow us. He was running back towards his house, taking a short cut. Our way was the long way round, cutting through the farm-house was by far the quicker route. My heart pounded in time with my feet.

I looked at Paul as we ran. 'The farmer,' I panted. 'He's going . . .'

'I know,' Paul told me. 'I know.' The look on his face was one of scared determination. It was virtually five years to the day before I saw it again, that time when he was being chased by Bob Moody and his mate St. Pierre.

We were clear of the yard, running through the gate, dashing across the track. The field in front of us looked so big, the bushes that concealed the ditch and our den seemed so very far away. But even if we made it that far we still had another field beyond that before we made it to the lane which led back into the village. The sun was so hot and I was sweating hard. There was no sign of the farmer yet. If we could get a good head start across the field . . . He was only an old man after all. But he hadn't exactly been slow in those massive galoshes of his, never mind in normal boots. We leapt clear of the track and started across the open field.

The mud of the field slowed us down. The hard, awkward lumps twisted our ankles, making us watch where we were putting our feet, making it so easy to stumble and fall. We had to slow down. Falling would be disastrous.

We weren't quite a quarter of the way across the field when the old man's shouts burst out of the farmhouse. Not far enough, I was telling myself. We're not far enough in front. I kept thumping my feet down one in front of the other. Paul turned to look over his shoulder. 'Oh, God!' I heard him say and I twisted my head to look.

Paul was hissing through his panted breath. 'He's got a gun! He's got a gun!'

The farmer was standing on the dirt track at the edge of the field. He was shouting at us. I saw him snap the two barrels closed and lift the dull metal gun to his shoulder. I have never been so frightened in my life. Before or after.

Both Paul and I were shouting now. I didn't know what I was shouting, it was just a way of releasing the painful fear that was burning inside me. I was shouting and running. My head was ducked low. I didn't have the wits to do anything else but run, no longer being careful with my feet, just slamming them down. I was running for my life.

I don't know what I heard first, whether it was Paul's scream or the bang from the gun. It could have been either. But whichever it was, Paul went down.

His leg went out from underneath him, twisting his body. He hit the ground hard and screamed like a baby. He writhed on the ground clutching the back of his left leg.

'I'm hit! I'm hit! He shot me!' The tears tumbled down his anguished face.

I stood staring stupidly. I didn't know what to do. It was as though I'd stopped running but everything about me was still going full tilt across the field. My head, my emotions, my sense were all halfway home now. The farmer was running towards us, his gun slung under his arm, but I simply couldn't move or think. The world had taken too sharp a detour off its normal route for me to have kept track of what was going on. We'd only been playing, I was telling myself. It was only a small den. The air was full of howls of pain and shouted curses. The sun was hot and bright.

I would have very probably stood there in a daze until the farmer had grabbed us both if I hadn't spotted the white pellet in the mud. I bent down and picked it up. It was about as long as a match but as fat as a candle and made up of solidly packed, tiny white cystals. It was a pellet of salt. And this had been what had hit Paul, not a proper bullet.

'I'm hit, I'm hit!' Paul cried, still squiriming on the mud.

'No you're not. Get up,' I told him. The farmer was getting too close for comfort.

'He shot me.' His face was red with pain.

'Not properly.' Now my brain was working again I realised it was obvious that the farmer wouldn't have used real bullets. 'This is what hit you,' I said showing him the salt pellet, desperate to get him to stand, the farmer getting closer and closer. 'This is what he shot you with, not a proper bullet.'

'It hurts!' Paul wailed.

'Come on, get up.' I tried to haul him to his feet. The farmer was only yards behind us.

Paul let go of his leg, biting his lip and making hissing noises, looking at his hands for signs of blood. I was switching my attention between the hulking form of the farmer and my friend's tentative movements, then at the hedges that surrounded the ditch. They were still at least the length of a football pitch away.

The farmer didn't seem to be slowing down. Paul was finding it difficult to stand. We weren't going to make it. He couldn't run with his leg feeling as though somebody had put a drill through it. But he was trying to stand. And the farmer was shouting. I could make it to the bushes on my own, I told myself. If I went now I'd be home free. Paul was clinging on to my arm, his face creased in agony, gasping for heavy shuddering breaths that couldn't stop the tears from spilling down his cheeks. I knew I couldn't leave him. I'd never leave him. But the farmer was almost upon us.

Paul had an arm around my shoulder. He was hopping on his good leg, I was holding him up. We were moving again, but so slowly it was painful. I had my arm around his waist, urging him on, trying to help him over the mud as much as possible. I ended up virtually dragging him towards the bushes.

The farmer was literally steps behind us, and gaining.

'Come on, Paul. Come on!'

I swear I could feel his hot breath on the back of my neck.

'I can't. I can't.'

The old man was within grabbing distance of us. But he fell. His ankle twisted on a large, boulder-like chunk of mud. He grunted as the wind was knocked out of him in an explosion of breath that I'm sure I felt rush past me.

We heard him fall but didn't turn round to look. The bushes were creeping closer and closer. I tried to push the thought away that even when we reached them we'd still only be halfway to safety, maybe less. That particular thought didn't bear thinking about.

Paul was heavy. Not only was I dragging him towards the bushes but he was also dragging me down. Maybe we shouldn't head towards the bushes after all. Maybe we should just get on to the lane as quickly as possible – it would be a lot easier to run on a road. And I was just about to say as much to Paul when I saw the police car, the sunlight glinting off the windscreen.

The farmer saw it too. He struggled to his feet and started waving his hands, shouting. The copper didn't see him however. We had the sun on our side; he would have had its glare in his eyes if he'd looked across the field. He drove all the way along the lane at the side of the field, all the way to the track that led up to the farmhouse.

The farmer didn't know what to do. He watched as we put more and more distance between him and us. Did he keep up the chase with us? Or did he get the police first? It took him only a moment's hesitation before deciding to go for the police.

It took us another two or three minutes to make it to the bushes. We dived straight into their cover, not caring about the nettles and sharp branches. Sweat was pouring off me; I had a stitch in my side and my shoulders and legs ached through keeping Paul on his feet.

'We've got to stop,' Paul said.

I nodded. 'I know.'

He didn't mean we had to stop because we were both exhausted, he meant that we'd now need to think of another plan to get away from here. Even if we made it as far as the lane now, we'd never be able to out-run a police car.

I slumped Paul up against a tree and peered through the tangled branches out across the open field. The farmer had made it back to his house and was waving his hands about in the copper's face, pointing back in our direction, stalking back and forth with a limp he must have gained with his fall. I noticed he wasn't carrying his gun any more.

'How's your leg?'

'It canes.'

'Let's have a look,' I said and stepped over to him as he tentatively dropped his jeans. The bruise was as big as a football. It was almost every colour of the rainbow; dark purple, orange and even a thick green around the edges, with thin, twisting threads of blood-red rippling out from the black centre spot where the pellet had actually hit him. 'At least it hasn't broken the skin,' I said.

Paul nodded, biting his lip. 'What're we gonna do?' he asked, hissing as he slowly eased his jeans back up.

I shrugged and peered out of the bushes again. 'I don't know, but we better think of something quick 'cos the farmer's getting in the cop car. They'll be driving along the lane any minute.'

'So we're trapped then.'

I nodded. 'We can't stay here. They're bound to find us if we do.'

'There is one way out,' Paul told me.

'I suppose we could head back to the farmhouse,' I said. 'You know, hope they keep going all the way in to the village and give us enough time to go right round the edge of the fields. We could come out on Postman's Walk, near the golf course.'

'There is a quicker way.'

I looked at Paul. He motioned towards the ditch. 'Follow it all the way under the lane,' he said. 'We'd still come out near Postman's Walk and it'd only take half the time. And we'd be hidden most of the way along, too.'

I nodded, it seemed to be the best idea.

I checked on the farmer one last time. He was in the police car, heading back down the track towards the lane. I helped Paul climb down into the deep ditch then jumped down behind him. Because the ditch was so narrow there was no room for me to help Paul along and we had to walk in single file. Luckily he was able to use the high sides to support himself, but it was still slow going. To be on the safe side we really wanted to be under the road before the farmer or the copper realised we hadn't kept on running towards the village. We made it as far as the two-plank bridge the farmer had dragged me across before we heard the police car shoot by towards the village.

'You okay?'

Paul nodded, his head hung low, his leg giving him problems.

'We can maybe rest when we get as far as the den,' I said. And then was suddenly and horribly struck by something we hadn't thought of yet.

Paul must have twigged on at the same time. He turned round and we both stared at each other. I closed my eyes and nodded, dreading what was coming.

The closer we got to the den the more horrible the smell became. It smelled as though the heat was baking it. We pushed past the low hanging branches at the bend in the ditch and saw the manure lying deep and filthy along what had originally been the dry bed, all the way up to the entrance of the den. It had slid down the sides of the bank from where the farmer had plastered it to lie even deeper still. It was going to come up way past our ankles. We could go no other way but through it; the bushes were too close to the top of the ditch for us to fight our way through them, and Paul would never be able to make the awkward climb with his leg anyway. It was going to be like walking through a swamp. A rank and fetid swamp.

'Give us a piggyback?' Paul asked with a grin.

'Stuff off,' I told him, although secretly I was pleased he could still joke at a time like this.

The smell was making me feel ill. The sludgy look of the stuff was disgusting.

'Maybe we can just wait here,' I said. 'They might not come looking for us.'

'They'll definitely not come looking for us if we go through that lot,' Paul said.

'What d' you mean?'

'They wouldn't believe we'd do it. They'd think only somebody really stupid would wade through there.'

'But you are really stupid.'

'Exactly,' he said.

I shook my head. 'I don't know, Paul. I don't think I can do it. What am I going to tell my mum? She'll go crazy. I don't know what's worse, getting covered in that stuff or getting caught by the farmer.'

'No way,' Paul said, shaking his head. 'No way am I gonna let that farmer catch me. Not now. Not after this.' He pointed at his leg.

'I'm not talking about giving up. I'm just saying that . . .'

But the argument came to an abrupt end when we heard the sound of a car pulling up on the lane only a few metres away. I went to speak and Paul quickly shushed me. We heard two doors open and shut, footsteps, the unmistakable tones of the farmer and what we guessed to be the copper's voice.

Paul whispered at me. 'They're gonna search these bushes. We've got to go now.'

Reluctantly, oh so reluctantly, I nodded.

It filled my trainers. It sucked at my ankles. It was foul. I had to place my feet carefully because it was so slimy underfoot, and there was no way I wanted to slip and sprawl in the stuff. There were flies everywhere and I tried to breathe shallowly, dreading the thought of swallowing one, only allowing myself slight intakes of breath against the smell. Paul had a harder time than me; at least I could lift my feet to walk, but he had to hobble, dragging his bad leg behind him.

We could hear the farmer and the policeman crashing about in the hedges and bushes around us. They shouted to one another, the farmer insisting we had to be near by.

I hesitated at the entance to the den. The mouth of the pipe was low, and quite narrow. Thick manure was daubed all around the rim. I had to duck down and steady myself with my hands on the inside of the concrete pipe to squeeze inside. We had always crawled inside before, but I refused to crawl now, although I still managed to smear my arms and back with the stuff. The air inside the pipe was dark and cool, but the smell was as strong as ever, trapped in the cramped space.

Paul followed me in. 'Maybe we should wait here until they've gone,' he suggested. 'They can't see us in here.'

I moved into the middle of the pipe where the shadows were deepest and where the farmer hadn't been able to reach with his spade. 'Next time you rescue me,' I said to Paul, 'make sure you've got a proper escape route planned.' I was trying to wipe the muck off me by scraping my arms against the concrete of the pipe.

'Next time you need rescuing make sure nobody's got a gun,' Paul said. Then added, 'In fact, make sure you rescue yourself.'

We'd waited in the shadows of the pipe for almost a quarter of an hour before the farmer and the policeman had given up looking for us, and then we had crawled out of the pipe on the opposite side of the lane. By then it felt as though the smell was ingrained in my skin.

It had taken most of the afternoon to reach Postman's Walk and the golf course beyond, Paul wincing every step of the way. We'd sneaked on to the course and had stripped off our jeans by the water-trap on the fairway leading to the twelfth hole. We'd thrown our socks away and washed the legs of our jeans and trainers as best as we could, or at least until we'd been chased away by a couple of old blokes in silly trousers.

Paul ended up telling his mum he'd twisted his ankle; it was a good excuse for the way he hobbled and when she examined him she hadn't looked high enough up his leg to see the bruise. The bruise which took over six weeks to disappear. And we'd never gone back to the den again; we'd wanted revenge on the farmer but had never dared get it.

The thing that stuck in my mind most about that day, however, was what Paul had said to me when we were making our way along the ditch towards Postman's Walk. He'd had tears in his eyes but had been trying to hide them behind a grin.

'You owe me one for this, Stonner,' he'd said. 'You know that, don't you? You owe me big time.'

Chapter Eighteen

I was sitting on my bed nursing my hand when my father knocked lightly at the door. It was seven o'clock in the evening. The cut on my palm was still weeping. I was listening to my brother's Bon Jovi album, trying to find a certain song. I was crying and I was scared. Not because of Bob Moody or St. Pierre, not because of how much Katie had hurt me, but because of my best friend and blood brother.

'Come in.'

He stepped through the door silently, hesitated for a second or two, then sat on the chair in front of my desk. He picked up a pencil and rolled it around between his fingers. 'How's it going?' he asked.

I shrugged.

'Your mother and I are going to the hospital in a few minutes. We thought Lynne and Dave could do with a bit of a respite, they've been with him all day, apparently. Do you want to come with us?'

I shook my head.

'Do you want to talk about it?'

Again, I shook my head.

I hadn't come straight home after leaving Katie's house. I'd wandered around for a while first. I'd gone past Tollbar Roundabout, then doubled back along Duke Street. I'd walked as far as Carvard Avenue, but not as far as the comp. I'd caught the 3C on the corner and hadn't got off until the far side of Stonner. I'd walked back into the village along the country lane that took me past the farmer's fields, his house and our old den.

'Your brother wanted me to pass on a message,' my father told me. 'He said to let you know that Bob won't pester you again, no matter how moody he gets. Does that mean anything to you?'

I nodded, surprised. It wasn't like Robert to go out of his way for me.

'Apparently he bumped into a mate of yours in town, and Robert and some of his friends from work sorted it out for you. I guess I shouldn't really ask what it's all about, should I?'

I shook my head, but knew my father had probably guessed what Robert had been talking about anyway.

As I'd expected, my mum had been angry with me for not going to the hospital earlier. She'd said I'd been selfish, and that it was by no means the way to treat a friend, especially not a good friend like Paul. My parent's concern had made me realise that Paul meant almost as much to them as he did to me. They'd spent the last five years listening to me talk about us both. I guessed they'd also shared in some way a lot of what the two of us had been through, good and bad.

My father came and sat next to me on the bed. He smelled of Old Spice. He'd received a bottle for Christmas every year since I'd been little. 'Your hand still playing you up?' he asked.

I nodded. 'Yeah. It hurts.'

'You know, Mum's right about letting the doctor look at it.'

'It's okay. It'll go soon.'

My mother had filled me in with a lot of the details of Paul's accident. He had been on his way to Jane Lois-Lane's house as I'd thought. He'd been on his bike because his father had suspended his driving privileges for a week. He'd been caught using the car without asking; yesterday, when he'd come to pick me up from the bus stop on Duke Street. He'd broken most of what could be broken in his body, the doctors had said, but they weren't too concerned about them because they could be mended. It was his blood they were worried about. Apparently there was something peculiar about his blood, something abnormal, although my mother didn't know what exactly.

My hand was very painful. I fingered the cut. I knew why it hurt so bad now. I knew why it was weeping.

'Paul's got a cut just like that, hasn't he,' my father said.

I nodded.

He toyed with the pencil in his hand. 'I had a friend like Paul once. We were at school together, even bought our first car together, sharing it. Silly really, because we could only ever go out together, and we got sick of the sight of each other in the end.' He gave a little regretful laugh which sounded more like a sigh. 'Boy, do I wish I knew where he was now,' he said. 'I haven't seen him for almost twenty years. You grow up, you get to my age, and you miss those sort of people. The ones you've only ever got happy memories of.'

There was a long silence between us. My father wanted so much to take my pain away, he would have done anything in the world to take it. He just didn't know how to.

'He might appreciate you being there.'

'Is he awake yet?'

'No. Not yet. Although the doctors say it's very possible he can still hear you if you talk to him.'

'He's not going to wake up, is he?'

'Chris, I . . .' My father shook his head slowly. 'I don't know, son. I really don't know.'

I wanted my friend back. I was like a petulant child. I wanted my friend back so badly. I wanted to scream and shout until he came back to me. I think my initial, emotionless response to the news of his accident had been shock. Shock and sheer stupidity. But now realisation was washing over me in waves, there was a whole tide of emotion now; as cold, as deep and as seemingly endless as any sea.

'What am I going to do if he doesn't wake up? What am I going to do if he dies?'

There were tears in my father's eyes. 'I really don't know, Chris.' He was trying so hard to be controlled in front of me. 'I wish . . . I wish I . . .' But he couldn't hold them back and we sat and cried together on the edge of my bed while Paul's coma took him further and further away from me.

'I don't ever want to grow up.'

I was alone in the house; my brother was out with friends, my parents were at the hospital. I had no idea whether or not what I was about to attempt would work, would help Paul, or if it was even possible. But so many impossible things had happened recently that I knew better than to dismiss the idea.

The doctors claimed they didn't know what was wrong with Paul's blood, but then they'd never asked me for my opinion had they? I'd tainted it, I was certain of that. I'd broken the friendship, broken the bond, and so tainted the blood. But I didn't think the doctors would believe me if I tried to explain. My mother had told me they were doing tests on him, taking loads of different samples, and if they couldn't figure out what was wrong they were going to pump some fresh blood into him, give him a transfusion. Which I knew didn't leave me with much time. I was worried it would flush my blood out of his system, and I knew that without my blood inside him he would be lost from me for ever.

I thought about the 'research' Paul had been so enthusiastic about. That was what held the key, I was sure of it. Something had happened there, something had opened up to prove that there was more to this power than fun and games. If I needed confirmation to believe that this power had been given for a reason then here it was, sitting in my lap, staring me in the face.

209

And after all, when it came down to it, I owed him one.

I was nervous. I stared at the cut on the palm of my hand, at the dull, colourless blood the wound was leaking. I remembered my mirror image in the patterned glass of Paul's bathroom window. Unhealthy or what? I thought to myself.

I closed my bedroom curtains, restraining the evening light. I lay back on my bed and closed my eyes. I reached out for Paul, I held out a mental hand, ready to catch hold of his mind, pushing all other thoughts aside. I let the blackness invade, let it wrap me up tight.

Chapter Nineteen

Slowly I opened my eyes. The huge, bright room was empty. I blinked, and then it was full.

Matty Harker said 'Hi' as he pushed past me through the crowd. He was talking to Batman. A kid called Welton from our year at the comp was teaching the Headmaster how to play 'Smells Like Teen Spirit' on an old guitar. It was the same guitar Paul had sold him in Year Eleven. Paul's dad was chatting up Meg Ryan. Bob Moody, Paul's Grandma Stewart (who's been dead for the past three or four years), Obi-Wan Kenobi and the guy who plays the drums for the Manic Street Preachers were involved in what seemed to be a heavy conversation. I had no idea what the debate was about.

I stood quite still, not at all sure what was happening. The room was maybe three or four times the size of our old school hall, and packed from bare white wall to bare white wall with faces I recognised.

I was dazed, bewildered, disorientated. Where was I? What the hell was happening? Had I flipped, was I going crazy? My confusion was so complete that the feeling was actually quite frightening.

I watched the people milling around me. Famous people, faces from school and Swift's. There were some I didn't recognise, but only a few. Just what they where doing here, and where exactly here was, I had absolutely no idea.

But then I spotted Jane Lois-Lane. She waved at me. She was talking to the real Lois Lane, and the pair of them looked a lot more alike than I'd ever given Jane credit for. And there was only one person who'd ever believed they could look so similar, similar enough to be at least sisters, if not twins.

I realised I was standing inside Paul's head, inside Paul's mind. Maybe not exactly physically, but somehow I'd managed to plug into his subconscious. I noticed that not every face in the room was an exact reproduction of their real-life counterpart. Paul's father, for example, was a lot bigger than I'd ever thought him to be. He looked a lot stronger and more domineering. Bob Moody was slightly altered in Paul's representation of him too. I'd always considered the guy to be fairly intelligent, which in my eyes had only made him even more dangerous, but this Bob Moody looked quite manic, verging on the downright insane.

And I know what you're thinking: I'm talking rubbish, right? But where else would you see Sting and our Year Ten Geography teacher chatting happily with Clint Eastwood dressed as The Man With No Name. It made me wonder what went on in my own head, who populated my own memory room, who populated anybody's? But then again, if you remember rightly, Paul had always been the one with the freaky imagination.

(I wondered if Katie was here, but refused to let myself look for her.)

While I was watching the faces in the crowd an electronic bell pinged tinnily somewhere over my head and the room fell silent. I looked around myself and all the faces were expectant, waiting.

'Nicole,' a voice announced, a voice I didn't recognise, one that I couldn't even sex as a matter of fact. 'Nicole, please.' And a door I hadn't seen before opened in the wall on the far side of the room.

The general hubbub resumed. But I wanted to see who Nicole was. I couldn't remember Paul ever mentioning a girl called Nicole, and I didn't think there'd been anybody at the comp by that name. I pushed my way past Robert De Niro and apologised to the DJ from Swift's when I bumped into him, heading for the door that had opened. Nicole was a slim girl, long, fair hair and a short dress, with legs that looked as though she'd used Mr Sheen on them.

'Every night,' she tutted in a French accent to Christopher Lambert dressed as the Highlander: sword, kilt, the full works. 'Sometimes two or three times.' And as the door closed behind her I realised she was the girl from the Renault Clio adverts.

At least the coma is still allowing him to dream, I thought.

The door Nicole had disappeared through had disappeared with her. I couldn't see any other doors anywhere. The high, wide walls were whitewashed and blank. Basically I didn't know what I was meant to be doing inside Paul's head now that I was here, but I had the feeling that I wouldn't be doing any good if I stayed in this room. I guessed I really should be heading deeper, the idea of which made me feel nervous all over again. These memory people all seemed pleasant enough, all quite polite as they chatted among themselves, but I didn't know what I was likely to encounter if I started exploring the darker recesses of Paul's mind. I knew the kind of scary thoughts he could have. I didn't want to come up against any of them.

I was thinking that maybe I should wait for someone else to be called through into his dreams and sneak through the door with them, when I spotted my own face in the crowd. I was a little shocked at first. I found the feeling of seeing myself like that was somehow quite disturbing. It wasn't like seeing myself in the mirror because I could see all of me, not just my head and shoulders. It was also different to seeing myself on video because I looked somehow *whole*. The only word I could use to describe how this image of me looked is 'touch-able'. I didn't recognise the person I was talking to, she was an older lady, maybe forty or so. She was blonde like Paul, a tall woman with a rather sharp face, but attractive all the same. I wondered if she was possibly an auntie of his, his mum's sister perhaps? He'd often talked about his Auntie Cath but I'd never actually met her in the real world.

The real world.

Was this real? Was I really inside Paul's mind, brought here by the power that was between us? Maybe this was a dream. Maybe when I'd laid down on my bed I'd fallen asleep and this was only an especially vivid dream. Maybe my father would wake me soon with news of his visit to the hospital.

I shook my head. I hoped not. I really hoped not.

I tapped myself on the shoulder. 'Er . . . Chris?'

I turned from my conversation with the middle-aged woman. 'Yes?' Then I recognised myself. 'Oh, hello.' I was wearing my favourite shirt, the one I'd worn to the pictures with Katie. My glasses looked a little skew-whiff, but I was pleasantly surprised to see that Paul's image of me was better-looking than the real me. I had a firmer jaw, and my eyes were darker, more masculine, more mature. I would have to remember to thank him.

'Sorry to interrupt,' I said.

'That's okay,' I told myself. (Did I really have such a nasal quality to my voice?)

'Er, listen . . . Chris. I'm not sure if you know why I'm here or not,' I said, 'but I was wondering if you knew how I could get out of here.'

'Out of where?' I asked.

I told myself to remember not to thank him for my lack of nous. 'Here,' I gestured with outstretched arms. 'This room. I really need to go deeper, you see.'

I nodded. But I swear the look on my face was one of feigned comprehension, and I wished I didn't know myself so well. 'The only door we ever use is the Dream Door,' I said. 'But there are two others.'

'Where?' Again I scanned the blank walls.

'They're only there when they're needed.'

I waited for myself to elucidate, but in the end had to ask: 'And what's behind them?'

'One is for The Forgottens,' I said, rather too melodramatically, even for me. 'No one has ever come back from there. I don't know where the third one leads, I've only ever seen it used once.'

'Once? And how long have you been here?'

'How long have I known Paul?'

'About five years,' I said.

'Then it's about five years,' I replied.

I had another question, but before I had time to ask it the electronic bell pinged tinnily above my head again. The vast room was silent and anticipation filled the air. The atmosphere felt something like the end of term assembly when the Headmaster gave out the sporting trophies and merit awards.

'Chris,' the sexless voice announced. 'Blood brother Chris, please.'

I looked at myself. And I looked back. A different door to the one Nicole had walked through opened on the opposite side of the room.

'Twice,' I told myself. 'That's twice now I've seen that door open.'

'Are you coming too?' I asked.

But I shook my head. 'No. That door's not meant for us.'

I nodded. Then something occurred to me. 'When was the last time you saw this door opened?'

'It must be almost five years ago now.'

'Was Paul's life in danger then?'

'Yeah. I seem to remember dens and running away from fat farmers with guns.'

'Who was called through the door that time?'

'No one,' I said. 'It was a false alarm.'

I nodded. I thought I was maybe beginning to get the hang of things. I took a deep breath. This was it then. I started to squeeze through the crowd. Agent Mulder was in my way and I shoved him aside thinking he'd be able to make one hell of an X-file out of this. I paused briefly to look back at myself. 'How often do you get called through the Dream Door?' I asked.

'Most nights,' I replied with a smile. 'Most nights.'

The crowd of memory people were silent as I made my way through them towards the door. They all watched me. It didn't help my nerves.

The door was little more than a rectangular hole in the white wall of the massive room. In fact there wasn't really a door at all, just an empty space. I hesitated before stepping through it. All I could see on the other side was darkness. It brought back memories of the pain I'd felt when Paul and I had been involved in our 'research'. I told myself that I should be able to trust Paul, however. I told myself that he would never do anything to harm his best friend, his blood brother. But I knew the kind of dreams I could sometimes have myself. I knew the terror of a nightmare and the clinging paranoia of waking in the dark. And I knew that he possibly could do nothing to help me anyway, that maybe it was the coma which was in control of him now.

I looked back at the silent crowd. I wanted to see myself. But I was lost in the sea of faces. I took a deep breath and stepped inside the darkness.

When I took that step everything had been dark, but now I could see. And there wasn't a ten foot beetle waiting for me, waiting to crush me in its mandibles, there wasn't even the Bogie Man. But a girl was standing in front of me. Just a girl.

She was naked. I blushed. She didn't seem to notice. She was taller than me and slim like a model, tanned. She had long hair, dark with tight, spiralling curls. I didn't want to look, but I simply couldn't help myself; her breasts were very large. 'Would you follow me, please?' she asked.

I turned and checked the door behind me. But there was only a wall. 'Where're we going?'

'Deeper,' she told me as she turned on her heel, and started down the long corridor that led away in front of us.

I looked for the door one more time, then followed.

The corridor was high and wide. The floor I walked on was covered in grass, smooth like a bowling green, and roses grew from the walls. Spaced at alternate intervals were pictures framed on the wall, one to my left, one to my right. Next to each picture was a door, proper ones with handles and hinges. But the girl was heedless of these, she didn't slow her pace as she continued down the corridor. I didn't watch her as she walked, I felt embarrassed. I didn't know why, I was certain it was only natural for an eighteen-year-old boy to have one or two naked women running around inside his head. But this was Paul's naked woman, not mine, and I made sure my eyes were averted. I wondered who the naked woman inside my head would look like, and the only girl I could think of was Katie. And that hurt.

Instead of Paul's naked woman I looked at the pictures on the walls. The first one on my right was an oil painting of a familiar looking boy aged about two or three sitting astride a large dog. Both the boy and the dog had almost clown-like grins splashed across their faces. Another on my left was a photograph of a boy (the same boy a year or so older, I realised) crying as he walked towards what looked like a school building. Behind him, far off in the distance, was his mother. She looked fluffy, all soft and cuddly. The school looked dark and ugly, dangerous like the jaws of a dragon.

I turned away from the pictures then, trying to see beyond the naked girl, trying to see our destination, but the corridor seemed to lead on and on.

'Hurry now,' the girl said.

I looked back at the pictures. There was one in a roughly circular frame that looked like a tie-dyed T-shirt and was as big as a football. It was almost every colour of the rainbow; dark purple, orange and even a thick green around the edges, with thin, twisting threads of blood-red rippling out from a black centre spot. I couldn't work out what these pictures were meant to signify until I saw the watercolour depicting the scene from Paul's bathroom when we'd become blood brothers. It was a perfect representation of the pair of us, with even our mirror images reflected against the patterned glass of the bathroom window. Paul was standing in front of me holding his right hand

219

out, palm up, his eyes closed. But Paul's memory of the event must have differed slightly from mine because I certainly couldn't remember either the cruel look on my face or the fact that the razor blade had been quite so large between my fingers.

It all seemed so long ago. So much seemed to have happened since then.

A picture to my left looked as though it had been drawn in wax crayon. It was a jagged blur of blue. It was scrawled and messy and I couldn't work out what it was supposed to be. I stopped and looked at it closely. I'd been with Paul virtually all of the time since becoming blood brothers, so surely this memory should match up with one of mine? But I simply couldn't make out what it was a picture of.

I looked at the next one along. But the frame was empty. Anxiety crawled like a spider along my spine, quick and skittery across my flesh, leaving goose bumps. The corresponding door was boarded up and padlocked. There were no more pictures after the blue scrawl, no more on either side. I noticed that the grass was brown beneath my feet, that patches of bare soil showed through. And the roses on the wall were limp and lifeless.

'Please hurry,' the naked girl said. She was holding open the door next to the blue scrawled picture for me.

'Why are there no more pictures?' I asked. The pit of my stomach felt all too hollow. I looked further up the corridor as it led away, still no closer to its destination.

'Because that's where they end,' she said without turning round. 'Step this way. Hurry please.'

I followed her motions towards the door without thinking. I hadn't noticed how dark or close the corridor had become. She was holding the door open for me, but I hesitated before I stepped through it. There was a certain smell in the air now, it was getting stronger and made my breath taste bitter at the back of my mouth.

'Please,' the girl said, plaintive as well as insisting. She was trying to usher me through that door, but wouldn't touch me.

'The pictures,' I said. 'I don't understand.' The atmosphere was suddenly oppressive in the corridor. There was no sound, the air was deathly quiet, but there was a pressure building up. It was as if the walls were being squeezed or crushed by massive hands.

The girl shook her head. She had a sore on her face. As I watched the raw inflammation spread across her cheek, the red skin cracked and split, black round the edges. I recoiled from her. She had sores on her neck, her shoulders, her belly. The floor of the corridor buckled behind her, the walls crumpled like a paper bag.

'Please.' There were pinpricks of tears in her eyes. The sores spread and cracked and burst. She looked like a burning photograph. The corridor and the pictures were crumbling, dissolving around us.

'Please, Chris.'

I stepped backwards through the door. It closed and disappeared into the shadows before my eyes, the image of the naked girl lost forever.

Everything was dark. I could feel the air around me. It was thick and heavy, restricting my movements, killing my dexterity. It was like walking through deep water. The sensation reminded me of the feeling of running in a dream; no matter how hard I had pumped my arms and legs I'd only ever been able to move bare inches, no matter how wildly I had flailed my body I'd never been able to escape the thing that had been chasing me.

And something *was* coming, something *was* following me. I could sense that whatever had destroyed the corridor and the girl with it was close behind me.

The memory of so many cold childhood nightmares came flooding back. The darkness seemed to cling to me and I stayed as still and as silent as I could. Just like I always had when I'd woken sweating and frightened in the middle of the night as a child.

Had all the others been wiped away too? Had Paul already lost his dream people?

I could hear something through the dark, something in the distance.

Desperate to steady my nerves I forced myself to look around. I peered into the blackness but could see no further than my own outstretched hand. There were no walls, no ceiling, no floor. I seemed to be suspended in the pitch, hung from the tethers of night. I plucked up enough courage to take a tentative step forward and proved that movement was possible, just, but slow and awkward. I knew I had to follow the sounds that were somehow managing to reach me and slowly, awkwardly, walked against the soft, spongy resistance of the dark.

With every step the noises got closer. There was a green light far off that pierced through the blackness, and occasionally a duller red or orange one. I focused on these lights like beacons, forcing my way towards them. I was sure that this was where the sounds were coming from. And the closer I got the more I came to believe that they were the sounds of engines, of traffic and cars.

My legs were heavy and cumbersome, the darkness wanting to drag me down. But I couldn't let it. It was like sludge tugging at my ankles, pushing against my chest and shoulders. I slogged my way on through it towards the changing lights. I concentrated on those lights. I refused to let my mind think about what was following me.

I don't know how far I walked, or for how long, but the blackness had all but sucked away my strength by the time I reached the traffic lights at the top of Town Road. The four-way intersection was big and brightly-lit before me, cars and lorries and motorbikes coming out of the pitch to cross the junction before fading away on the other side. I was trembling slightly with the effort of the walk, exhausted, my breath short and heavy. I wanted to sit down but was scared that if I did the dark would drag me down and pull me under. I leaned up against one of the winking lights as it went through its cycle of red, amber and green to try to get my breath back. I bent at the waist, my hands on my knees and breathed deeply. But even then I was fighting against the blackness as it piled its weight on my back, trying to buckle my knees and push me down.

It would be so easy to let it, I thought to myself. It would be so very easy to succumb and lie down within it.

I tried to push the thought aside. I forced myself upright, feeling the weight of the darkness slide off my back and watched the traffic. I had to be here for a reason. Paul must have led me here on purpose.

And then I saw him. He was on his bike; his old, battered racer with the loose saddle and buckled front wheel. He was coming along Town Road from the direction of where Cleeston would be in the real world. He was standing up on his pedals, pushing as if against an unseen wind. He was wearing his Walkman and was singing to himself. I called out to him, but he couldn't hear me, the dark was all too eager to snatch away my words. So I sent to him with my mind, and still he didn't respond.

He cast a quick glance over his shoulder and then moved into the centre of the road without signalling. He was going to turn right into Taylors Avenue. The light was on red and he began to slow down. I got ready to step out into the road to greet him, although he still hadn't seen me yet. But then before he had time to stop, the light changed and Paul pushed down on his pedal, moving into the middle of the junction to turn the corner. He didn't see the blue Rover as it shot the light to his left.

'Paul!' I yelled. 'Watch out!' But the shadows gagged me.

I watched in horror as the car didn't even slow, didn't even swerve. It hit him with a palpable crunch of metal and bone. His old racer went under the front of the car, Paul was slammed backward onto the bonnet. The Rover's front end bucked slightly as it churned the bicycle underneath its wheels, sparks flew from the road. Paul hit the windscreen with a loud crack and was flipped, tossed over the roof, his arms and legs like the limbs of a rag doll. His head lolled and jerked.

224

There was the screech of brakes, a horn bleared and the other cars on the road skidded to a halt. Paul hit the tarmac of Town Road behind and to the left of the blue Rover. He crumpled up on himself, rolled once, then lay still. His bike was trapped under the Rover's front wheels, twisted and broken.

I closed my eyes against it. My stomach churned and I thought I was going to be sick. I couldn't move. I wanted to run out to him but I simply couldn't move. I took deep breaths trying to calm myself down. I was shaking terribly. I clasped my hands tightly together to try and control it.

But when I managed to force my eyes open again Paul had gone. The accident had disappeared. The traffic flowed freely across the junction. I stood bewildered, looking about myself. I couldn't understand . . .

But suddenly there he was again, standing up on his pedals, glancing over his shoulder, moving out, into the centre of the road.

'No!' I screamed. 'No!' I made a dash towards him but the darkness was so thick around me, was pulling me back. I waved my arms. The blue Rover moved into view. – No, Paul, no! –

And I turned away from it, turned my back on the sickening rythmn of the accident as it happened all over again. The grinding of metal, the crack of the windscreen, the screech of the tyres.

And no sooner had the noise died away when it started again. Paul ploughing against the wind, Paul slamming against the bonnet, and crumpled on the tarmac.

And again.

I held my hands to my ears, I tried to block out the deafening sounds. But the noises were inside my head. I shouted and screamed against them, yelling until my lungs burned. I clamped my hands to my ears and could still hear it so loud.

And again. The grating crunch of metal, the startled blare of horns.

Why is this happening? Please stop. No! It hurts. Please . . .!

And again.

– You owe me one –

I looked up. For a split second, the briefest of moments, I saw a sparkle of recognition in Paul's eye. But I didn't know what to do. I didn't know how to help. I was a frightened child in a nightmare I could not wake from. I fought with tears of frustration.

But the darkness began to shimmer in front of me. I could smell something bitter around me. I saw the black pitch of night turn hazy, inconsistent. Its weight was suddenly lifted from my shoulders. The road shook beneath my feet, I saw a lamppost bend, a curb buckle and break. I knew then that the force from the corridor had caught up with me, and with that realisation came another. I knew what it was, I knew what was chasing me. It was the fresh blood the doctors were giving him, the transfusion. My blood was being forced out of Paul's body, my presence out of his mind. It wasn't trying to harm Paul, it was after me, I was the one it needed to eliminate.

I had to act fast. I ran into the road. The dark was feeble and weak around me because of the disruption. Without its presence I could move so much easier. It still tried to cling to my limbs in thick ribbons, it still groped at me as I ran, but it was nowhere near as strong as it had been.

– Paul! get out of the way –

I dodged in between the cars. A Volkswagen missed me by the breadth of a hair. A Capri scraped at my backside. I kept my eyes on Paul. I saw the Rover moving quickly out of the darkness and on to the road.

– Paul! –

I had my head down, my arms pumping madly but my feet coming down slower and slower as the black gained a better grip on me the further I moved into the road. The road felt soft beneath me, sucking, pulling me down. An Escort winged my side. The pain was a sharp explosion, it felt as if something inside had burst. I was nearly knocked down. I stumbled through the spongy air, desperate to keep my feet and roared at the hurt.

The Rover drew closer. It was moving so much quicker than me. I saw the traffic lights twist and snap behind me. The pavement and gutter cracking, tearing open.

– Please, Paul! Look! –

The Rover changed lanes. Paul pushed on his pedals to move away from the lights.

– No, Paul, no! –

But Paul was oblivious, his mouth moving to the tune on his Walkman, his eyes already round the corner he was turning. The Rover's course was set for destruction. I tried to run again. The air was so stagnant. It would not move to let me pass.

– PAUL –

I charged in to him with my shoulder, pushing him backwards, tipping him from his bike. It skittered into the centre of the junction. Paul fell into a heap on the road. The Rover sped on, smashing the cycle's frame beneath its wheels. I tumbled and rolled across the white lines on the tarmac, the road was crumbling away beneath me. There was the sound of horns, cars screeching to a halt. But the road had already shattered and I was falling through it.

Chapter Twenty

And then I woke up.

For the second time in as many mornings I woke to the sound of the phone ringing. I lay still and quiet and waited for someone to answer it. I had a terrible pain in my side.

'Chris,' my mother called. 'It's for you.'

Gingerly I climbed out of bed and headed downstairs. My mother was standing in the hall clutching the telephone's receiver, her hand clasped over the mouthpiece.

'It's Paul's father,' she mouthed at me, then hovered by my shoulder to hear what was said.

'Hello?'

'Hello? Hello, Chris? It's Dave, Paul's dad.' He sounded nervous and excited. His words were fast and they all rolled into one another.

'What's he say?' my mother asked. 'Is there any news?'

'We, that's his mum and I . . . We thought you'd want to know, he's awake, he's fine, they gave him a transfusion early this morning and everything's okay, he's doing well. I . . .' He took a much needed breath. 'He woke about an hour ago, Doctor said he's doing fine. And he asked about you. Lynne, his mum, she said to ring you, let you know. But he's doing well. Really well. Do you want to pass on a message?'

I looked at the cut on the palm of my right hand. It had scabbed over quite opaquely. 'Tell him we're equal,' I said. Then smiled and changed my mind.

'No,' I said. 'Tell him: Super Stonner to the rescue.'

'She's nice though, don't you think?'

'She's a *nurse*, Paul.'

'Exactly. Even better, yeah?'

'But, she's . . . Oh, forget it. So how much longer are they keeping you in?'

'Not sure. They're still messing about with tests and stuff on my blood. I'm an anomaly.'

'Doesn't surprise me.'

'But I haven't told them anything. You know, about you and me, and what we did and stuff.'

'Best not to.'

'It did happen though, didn't it?'

'Well, I . . . Well, yeah, I guess so.'

'Good, I hoped it had,' he said.

He smiled sweetly at the nurse as she walked by, his eyes following her for the length of the ward, then he grinned up at me mischievously.

'Betcha can't guess what I'm thinking.'

'Betcha I don't want to,' I told him.

ALSO BY KEITH GRAY

Creepers

Derwent Drive was known as the Speed Creep. And it was certainly the speediest Creep around here. You had to move so fast, most of the way along you didn't have time to think. It was a continual chain of Dashes into Blind. We'd all heard the story about the Creeper who'd dropped Blind into a garden, only to discover he was standing in a dog pound with five alsatians all around him. It was also famous because it was the longest creep in the village; twenty-five houses all in a row, from Number Two to Number Fifty, no bends, no kinks. Just straight and Speedy. And not one Creeper had ever done the lot. If we could make it to the end, make it all the way to Number Fifty, we'd hold the record, we'd be the best. And Jamie and I reckoned we could do it. Jamie was the best Speed Creeper around. He was the best Buddie you could have. And he was mine.

A brilliant first-novel about friendship, courage and loss.

'A powerful and original young writer. By the time I'd finished the book, I wanted to go on a Creep myself.'
Gillian Cross